REMNANTS OF THE DEAD

Realm Of The Dead: Book 5

Jeremy Dyson

DARTMOOR
PUBLISHING

Dartmoor Publishing

CONTENTS

For Sarah

CHAPTER ONE

This is it. Once we do this there is no going back. I watch the guards circling in their towers above the yard of the prison and get the unshakable feeling that something bad is about to happen.

"Scout," I whisper. "What do you see?"

Scout lowers the binoculars from her eyes. Her face is suddenly pale. I notice the hair on her arms standing up even though the autumn afternoon air is warm. Something about the question or just the sound of my voice spooks her somehow.

"Do you see Stevie?" I ask her again.

Her tongue wets her lips, and then she turns her head and looks in my direction. Her gaze isn't focused on me, but instead, it's like she is looking right through me at something in the distance. When her eyes finally settle on my face, she appears confused for a moment. She even seems a little scared. It's like she is staring at ghost or something like that. Scout swallows to clear her throat.

"He might not be there," Scout says. "I don't see him."

She grabs her pack and shoves the binoculars back into the front pocket and zips it closed. The color begins to return to her face again as she regains her focus.

"Are you sure?" I ask her.

"I said I didn't see him, Steven!" she snaps.

Scout stops moving for a moment when she realizes her mistake. She lets out a heavy sigh and brushes the loose strands of hair out of her face before she picks up her backpack and slides her arms through the straps.

"Hey," I say. "It's okay."

"I'm sorry, Blake," she says. "I just—"

"You don't have to explain yourself to me," I say.

"What do you want to do now, Scout?" Fletcher asks.

Scout twists around to look at him but doesn't answer. Instead, she thinks about it while she stares at the fences surrounding the prison in the distance.

"I didn't come all this way for nothing," Scout says.

My eyes scan the yard outside the facility again. Guards with rifles stationed in the towers watch over a crowd of prisoners in the dusty trodden field below. It looks like there may be close to a hundred prisoners being held here by the Reapers.

"Okay then," Tim says. "We should make our move now."

"You don't want to wait until dark?" I ask him. "So, we have some cover."

"No," Tim shakes his head. "If we come at them this way, with the sun behind us, it will leave them looking into it. They'll be blind. That will give us enough time to get the upper hand."

I glance back into the bright sun and squint my eyes. Tim is right. It burns my corneas to stare into the light for more than a second.

"We need to move now, though, or else we'll lose our advantage."

I'm still not sure about this. I have to wonder if we are making a mistake. My eyes keep going back to the prison. From this distance, I can't make out how many more guards we might have to deal with, but I would guess we are probably outnumbered.

"Blake," Scout says. "You with us?"

I notice everyone else is ready to move already. They stand there looking at me with their guns gripped tightly in their hands. I must have been staring at the prison for longer than I realized.

I almost say something, but then I look at Scout again and spot something familiar in her determined expression. It's a look I've seen before when I looked into the mirror and told myself that I would not give up until I found my daughter. Nothing I say could possibly stop her from going in there to look for him.

"I'm with you," I say.

Even though I still think this is too risky, I won't let them go without me. I owe them that much and I know they would do the same for me. The same way Quentin and Danielle risked their lives to help me look for Abby in Chicago. I owe it to them, too.

"Well, let's get going then," Fletcher says.

I push myself up off the ground and check my rifle to make sure it's ready before I crouch down and follow the others out of the woods and into a meadow of long grasses and dying wildflowers. The vegetation is not high enough to fully conceal us, but if we keep low to the ground, we can easily avoid detection.

The scent of death suddenly overpowers the other smells of the earth. My eyes search the field uneasily and I turn my head to check back the way we came, but there is no sign of the dead. Then I hear my foot squishing in something that feels like mud beneath my boot.

Except it isn't mud.

I look down at the decomposing body of a man on the ground. At least, I think it was a man. Wild animals and time have consumed the flesh so it's impossible to tell for sure. My boot rests in a pile of rotting brain matter and swarming maggots spilling from a gaping wound to the skull of the corpse. The kind of hole made by a high-powered rifle.

There is no way to tell if he was already dead when the bullet put him down. Doesn't really matter either way, I guess. I free my boot from the muck and continue forward toward the fences. My body casts a long shadow onto the rocky soil. At moments like this, I feel less in control of my fate and more like I am being pulled along by the dark distorted figure that lives in the ground.

Something brushes against the side of my leg, and I glance down to see Stitch. He rushes ahead of me, weaving his way through the tall grass. Every so often, he pauses and turns back to check on us. The dog points his black nose to the sky and his nostrils flare as he sniffs the air and his tail wags.

I don't know how he can distinguish the walking dead from the decaying bodies on the ground, but he can.

Right now, it isn't the dead we need to fear.

The people inside the barbwire fences of the prison yard are being held by a group of criminals calling themselves the Reapers. It was the Reapers that infiltrated the government facility beneath Cheyenne Mountain.

They are led by a drug lord named Gustavo Castillo. Up until he was arrested five years ago, Castillo was head of the Juarez cartel. I know this because Tim was there. His special forces unit was involved in Operation Dark Shadow, a covert mission that took down Castillo and his entire operation.

These days Castillo goes by the name La Parca. Once the authorities lost control of the supermax penitentiary in Florence, La Parca seized upon the opportunity to organize the most dangerous convicts on the face of the earth and build himself an empire.

Most of what we know about the Reapers we learned from Bones. She used to be one of them. It wasn't like she had much of a choice. After she lost everything, she didn't know what else there was to be anymore. I can't say I blame her.

Focus, Blake.

Tim halts suddenly and raises a fist in the air. The rest of us stop in our tracks. Tim holds open his fingers and lowers his hand before he crouches lower to the ground. I drop to a knee and wait while Tim raises his rifle and scopes the facility again.

A few months ago, these combat hand signals would have meant nothing to me, but now I know exactly what they mean; *don't move... stay low.*

A guard in the nearest watchtower raises a hand to shield the light from his eyes. A suppressed shot rips through the air as Tim fires the rifle. The first guard falls as I hear a second shot. I glance over to the next tower and discover the other guard is gone as well.

We rush forward toward the fences again. Inside the prison yard, the people are all looking around for the source of the gunshots. Tim stops for a moment and crouches on one knee as he raises his rifle again. A second later, he squeezes the trigger and drops a guard aiming a rifle on top of the last watchtower.

Alarms blare.

Chaos takes over.

My heart pounds in my chest as I get up and start running toward the prison.

The doors to the nearest cell block burst open and half a dozen men with assault rifles rush the yard.

"Get the fuck on the ground!" one of them yells.

A few of the captives obey the order, but others panic and run away at the sight of the guns.

The guards aim their weapons at the prisoners while their eyes search the yard to try and figure out what is happening.

One man in filthy khakis and a flannel shirt with the sleeves cut off tries to charge the guards with a rock. The man stops suddenly and collapses on the ground. The sound of gunfire reaches me a split second later.

The distraction allows us enough time to get to within range. By the time the guards notice us on the other side of the fence and raise their palms to block the evening sun it's too late.

"Drop the guns!" I yell, even though I already know they won't listen. At least they were given a chance. That's more than most people get anymore.

Two of the guards move to raise their assault weapons, but a hail of bullets from our rifles stops them. Only one of the reapers even manages to pull the trigger, firing several rounds into the dirt as he collapses to the ground. The crowd of prisoners rushes the guards. They throw fists and kick at the bleeding men on the ground as they pry their weapons away from them.

Several shots are fired from within the facility, and I retreat to the concrete wall next to the door to find cover beside Tim. One of the prisoners holding a rifle is hit several times in the chest. The man lowers his head and stares at the bloody holes in his green sweater in disbelief. He lifts his head slowly and stares into the open doorways of the facility for a second before another bullet pierces through the top of his skull and he collapses on the ground.

The rest of the hostages scramble out of the line of fire as more gunshots ring out and bullets fly through the open doors and tear through the dirt and the bodies on the ground.

A man with an unruly beard and deep wrinkles in his leathery skin dives against the wall behind me. Tim peers around the corner and fires off a few rounds. He ducks back just as more gunfire from the inside sends a barrage of bullets back down the hall. Tim looks around me at the bearded prisoner.

"How many more of them are in there?" Tim asks him.

The man gasps and struggles to speak.

"A bunch of them," he finally manages.

Shouts can be heard inside followed by more gunfire.

"Give me a number," Tim demands.

"Thirty," the man yells over the gunfire. "Forty. Maybe more. I don't fucking know, man."

Tim grimaces. I don't think he was expecting that many.

In the afternoon, we watched several vehicles arrive and depart from the facility. We knew there would be more of them inside. Judging by the way Tim just flinched, I think that forty was even more enemies than he feared.

He leans around the doorway and fires into the hallway for several seconds before getting behind cover again and changing to a fresh magazine. Howls of pain and cries for help can be heard inside. On the opposite side of the doorway, Fletcher nods to his brother. Then the two of them rush inside.

I follow the two brothers inside with my rifle ready to fire. I can barely see around Chuck and Tim in the narrow hallway, but I glimpse shapes moving up ahead in the dim light.

"Don't even think about it asshole," Fletcher says. He rushes ahead with his gun pointed at the dark figures on the floor.

"Don't shoot!" A long-haired man at the end of the hall raises one bloody hand in the air. His other hand is pressed against his abdomen to stem the bleeding where he was shot. A woman lies on the ground beside him. Her long dark hair in a glistening puddle of crimson on the concrete floor.

Fletcher keeps his rifle trained on the man as he picks up a weapon lying on the ground nearby and passes it back to me. Tim crouches down and checks the woman for a pulse.

"She's still breathing," he says.

"Bones!" I turn and call back down the hallway.

The former autopsy technician pushes her way through the crowd near the entrance and hustles down the hallway. She crouches down beside the woman on the ground and unzips the duffel bag of medical supplies.

"They locked themselves inside," Fletcher says.

I look up to see where he is standing next to a closed steel door.

"Is there another way in?" Tim asks the dark-haired man on the ground.

"They already locked down the main entrance," the man says. "You'll never get in there."

"How many more men are inside?" Tim asks him.

The man hesitates. He hisses in pain and stares down at the blood trickling through his fingers. Tim grabs the man by the wrists and pulls his hand away from his abdomen. Blood gushes from the wound.

"You can tell me, or I swear to God almighty I'll make sure you bleed to death right here."

"Please, don't..." the man pleads.

"Tell me," Tim growls.

"Ten," the man says.

"Don't bullshit me," Tim warns the bleeding man.

"I'm not," the man tells him. "They sent the rest of us out this morning, I swear."

Tim releases his hold on the man and his hand clamps back over the wound again. Then Tim turns his head and looks at the woman on the floor. Her open eyes stare at an empty spot on the ceiling. Bones swipes her hand over the girl's face and closes her eyes. It was something I'd seen done in films a thousand times before, but this is the first time I can recall seeing someone do it since the dead stopped dying.

Finally, Bones lets out a sigh and stands up. She unholsters her pistol and fires it once. The shot rings loudly off the concrete walls.

Tim returns his gaze to the other man.

"How long until the rest of them return?" Tim asks.

"Please, help me," the man looks at Bones.

Bones and Tim exchange glances. Tim nods slightly to tell her she can start treating the injured man. She crouches down beside him and gets to work.

"How long?" Tim says again.

"They have a radio inside," the man says. "Probably called for help already. Going to be a lot more coming now."

"Shit," Fletcher curses.

Tim glances up at his brother and then returns his stare to the man on the floor.

"When?" Tim says.

"An hour," the man coughs. "Maybe two at the most."

Tim stands up, staring down at the man for a moment.

"We need to move," Tim says.

"I need to get the bullet out," Bones says.

"No time," Tim tells her.

"I just need a few minutes," she says. She reaches into her medical bag and pulls out a long clamp.

"Hold on," Scout says. I glance over my shoulder to find her standing in the hallway too.

"He's going to bleed out," Bones says. "I have to do this now."

"Wait," Scout says. "He is going to pass out and I need to ask him a question first."

Scout kneels beside the man.

"I'm looking for a kid," she says. "Red hair. About this tall she says." Scout holds a hand up to show him the approximate height of Stevie.

"I don't know, lady," the man says. "If he isn't out there, they might have taken him to the medical building."

"Where?" Scout says.

"Trust me, you don't want to go there, lady," he pauses to take a pained breath.

"Where is it?" Scout growls.

"Just outside the north fence," the man says. "Brick building."

Without a word, Scout stands up and heads back down the hallway.

"Wait up, Scout," Fletcher says. He shoulders his rifle and hurries to catch up with her.

Tim looks down at Bones again.

"Five minutes," he tells her.

She nods and gets ready to extract the bullet.

"You have no idea what you started," the man says. His bloodshot eyes stare at Tim even though he struggles to keep his head raised.

Bones probes inside his abdomen with her forceps instrument and the man yells. His whole body seizes up and his eyes roll back into his skull as he passes out from the sudden overwhelming pain. Bones adjusts the angle of the instrument in her hand and half a minute later she removes it along with the bullet and bunch of blood.

"Shit," she says. She tries to put pressure on the wound, but within moments the rag is soaked with blood and the man is dead. Bones picks up the rag and tosses it aside in frustration.

"Damn it," she curses. She stares down at the bodies on the floor for a moment.

"Come on," I tell her and reach out to help her up by pulling her arm. "Nothing you can do now. Let's go."

She reluctantly gets to her feet and wraps her bloody fingers around the handle of her pistol. Bones points her weapon at the man's head and squeezes the trigger. The echo of the gunshot seems to never end as we head for the dwindling daylight at the end of the hall.

CHAPTER TWO

"We can't stick around here," I say to Tim.

"I know," he says. He looks down to make sure he doesn't trip over the body on the floor.

We emerge from the doors of the cell block to find the crowd of prisoners gathered around the doorway in the twilight. Tim turns his head, one brow raised, as though he is trying to figure out why all these people are standing around looking at him. Maybe he is just trying to figure out where Scout and Fletcher went.

"What's the problem?" Tim asks the prisoners.

A murmur passes through the crowd.

"What are you all still doing here?" Tim asks no one in particular.

Many of the heads in the crowd turn to look around. Finally, an older man with his hand resting on the shoulder of a teenage boy beside him clears his throat.

"Mister," he finally says. "You see, we don't have anywhere to go."

"What do you mean?" Tim says. "Go anywhere you want. You can't stay here. It's not safe. The Reapers are on the way here right now. You all need to leave."

None of them move. They just stand there like a bunch of sheep waiting to be herded.

"Maybe we can go with you," the man finally says.

"With us?" Tim says.

"You must have some kind of safe place," the man says.

Tim glances at me. I can tell he never considered what we would do about the rest of the prisoners here once we took it over. None of us did. All we were trying to do was find Stevie.

"Look," Tim says. "You're all free now. *Free*. You can go wherever you want."

The older man takes a few steps forward and clears his throat again.

"It seems to me that we'd be smart to work together," the man says softly. "We can help. We can fight. But without food or weapons, we don't stand a chance on our own out there. But together... maybe we can build something."

Tim looks around at the gaunt faces of the prisoners.

"I'm sorry," Tim tells the older man and shakes his head.

"Son," the man grabs Tim by the arm. "Many hands make light work. Did you ever hear that? Think this through."

"He has a point, Tim," I say.

Tim shoots me a glance and pulls his arm away from the man. He stands back and folds his arms across his chest as he mulls it over.

From a numbers standpoint, it seems like we would have a much better chance of surviving if we had more people around. Some of them probably even have useful skills or training. We might need them.

"We didn't come here for this," Tim says, looking at me, then he returns his attention to the older man. Their eyes lock for a long moment before Tim scans the faces of the other prisoners.

"I'm not going to tell anyone here what to do. You're free, you understand? You don't need someone like me to tell you what to do anyway."

His words are met with murmurs and confused expressions.

"It's not ever going to be like it was before," he tells them. "If you want to live, you have to look out for yourself. You can't count on anyone else running your life anymore. The sooner you all figure that longer you will survive."

I hear the crickets chirp in the silent twilight when Tim pauses.

"Some of the Reapers are still alive inside and I'm sure that more of them are on the way," Tim says. "You need to leave. It isn't safe for you here."

The people whisper amongst themselves as the crowd disperses. They scramble to gather up what few belongings they have left to bring with them.

"This ain't right," the older man says. "Being out there on our own is just as bad as being in here. Maybe worse."

"You can keep the weapons and ammunition," Tim tells him. "This is Colorado. There are plenty of places in the mountains where you'll be safe. Stay off the main roads. Avoid any big cities. If you do that, you should be okay."

He claps the man on the shoulder and turns his back on the man and starts to walk away. The old man stares at Tim for a moment before he gives up and decides to leave.

"Are you sure about this?" I ask Tim.

Tim doesn't answer my question, but I can tell from his expression that he has already made up his mind. He looks back to the doors of the prison where Elise is holding her submachine gun across her chest and standing guard.

"Let's round our people up," Tim tells her. "We should get the hell out of here."

"I can go find Fletcher," Elise volunteers.

"Nah, I'll get him," Tim says. "Just make sure everyone else is ready to go when I get back."

Tim starts to walk away, and I decide to tag along and go look for Scout and Fletcher with him. I'm sure he doesn't need or even want my help, but something about the way he refused to help the rest of the prisoners troubles me. It seems like we might need their help.

I have been through a lot with Chuck, but I have only known his brother for several days now. With everything else going on, I really haven't talked to him very much yet. He took us in, so I know Tim is kind. He seems reserved and thoughtful, especially compared to his brother Chuck, who never seems to know when to shut up. I suspect his serious demeanor might have to do with the fact that he recently became a father and the struggle of raising a child in this world weighs heavily on his mind.

"You probably think I'm making a mistake," Tim says before I even open my mouth to say a word. He glances back over his shoulder at me as he crosses the prison yard.

"The thought crossed my mind," I admit.

Tim returns his gaze to the brick building in the distance.

"Go on," he says. "Let's hear it."

"I'm not saying I disagree with you," I tell him. "I'm just not sure I understand. It seems like we might be better off if we had more people to help us."

"Safety in numbers," Tim says. "That sort of thing?"

"Yeah," I say. "Something like that."

"Blake," Tim says. "If you want to be in charge of all those people, take care of them and make sure there is enough food for everyone, keep them safe, then go right ahead. Because if that's what you think is the right thing for you to do, I'm not going to stop you."

When he puts it like that, it sounds like more responsibility than I would want, too. I don't even say anything in response to him because I'm not sure what to say. He pauses and turns his head so that his dark green eyes meet mine.

"Heck, it probably is the right thing to do," Tim says. "But I got a family to worry about. You get me?"

"Yeah," I say. "But what about the Reapers?"

"What about them?" he says.

"Eventually we're going to have to deal with them," I say. "We can't take them on alone."

Tim comes to a stop suddenly. At first, it makes me think there must be trouble, but then he lets out a deep sigh. His eyes gaze at the last sliver of the setting sun peeking out from the mountain peak on the horizon.

"Here's the thing," Tim says. "I'm not looking to take anyone on, Blake. Especially not them."

His eyes lock with mine, and I notice his breath hanging in the chilly mountain air. It reminds me just how close we are to winter in the mountains.

"You know what kind of monsters they are," I say. "Are we really just going to hide in the mountains and do nothing while things like this happen?"

"I'm not hiding," Tim says.

"What do you call it then?" I ask him.

"I'm protecting the people that matter to me. You're right about one thing; I have seen what happens to the people that take these guys on," Tim says. "It ain't pretty, Blake."

He turns and starts walking toward the medical building again. His eyes stare down at the untended trodden grass as we pass by another decomposing body on the ground.

"Maybe you're right," I admit.

"It's not about being right," Tim says. "It's about being alive."

We walk up the steps and open the door. The overpowering scent of rotting bodies hits me. I have to take a step back from the door and cover my nose. The nauseating smell turns my stomach so much it feels like someone just punched me in the gut. The dead have a horrible smell, but this is something much worse.

"You alright?" Tim asks me.

I nod my head and then we push ahead into the darkened foyer. The intake area is empty. Loose papers flutter on the floor. Streaks of dried blood on the tile floors go through the open security door and to a doorway down the hall. It looks like a trail left behind by a body being dragged along the ground.

"Chuck!" Tim calls out.

"We're back here," comes a faint response from down the hall.

This building gives me a bad feeling. I sure hope Stevie was never in here.

"Come on, Scout," Fletcher pleads.

We walk down the hall, following the sound of Fletcher's whisper and the streaks of blood on the floor. Even though I don't really want to look inside the exam rooms, I can't seem to stop myself. Luckily, it is already too dark to see what lies in the corners, but the moonlight coming in through the slim window slits reveals enough of the horror.

A severed hand rests on the middle of the floor in the first exam room. Across the hall, a body decomposes on a gurney in the other room. The remnants of withered intestines dangle just above a collection of colored candles on the gore-splattered floor. In the next room, surrounded by more candles, is a small figurine of a skeleton dressed in robes and holding a scythe, like some sort of altar. A toppled bucket sits on the floor with a distinctive round bone-white shape resting beside it.

"What the fuck were they doing in here?" I ask Tim.

"Human sacrifices," Tim says.

"Sacrifices?" I say.

"To her," Tim says. He gestures to the statue.

"Her?" I say. "The Reaper?"

"Santa Muerte," he says. "Top narcos in the Juarez cartel have long believed that she watches over them... that she gives them power."

"That's crazy," I shake my head.

"People have always believed crazy shit. Believing crazy shit is practically a part of human nature."

We find Fletcher and Scout in the last exam room. Scout stares at the remains of several hacked-up bodies beside a cauldron filled to the brim with blood. Tears stream down her cheeks.

"He wasn't here," Fletcher consoles Scout. "Come on."

"We need to get moving," Tim agrees.

"We're coming," Fletcher says.

Scout allows him to usher her back out to the hallway that is almost pitch black now in the darkness. I can't get out of this place fast enough. In the last six months, I have seen so many gruesome things. The dead are capable of unthinkable horrors. But I have never come across anything like this.

We exit the building to find Stitch waiting outside. He wags his tail slowly as he jogs to Scout. Sometimes the dog seems like he knows exactly who could use his company, and sometimes he acts like a moron. Scout crouches down to pet him and he climbs on her knee and licks the side of her face.

"We'll keep looking," she whispers. "We'll find him."

The dog continues to lick her cheek and wags his tail some more. I exchange glances with Fletcher and Tim while we wait for Scout. None of us feel very optimistic that we will find the kid after what we've seen today, but I think we all know that Scout won't be giving up anytime soon.

I can't help thinking about my daughter Abby. I've been down this road before. I hate to say it, but I know where it will most likely lead us if we keep looking.

"Scout," Fletcher says.

"I'm coming," Scout tells him.

We meet up with the rest of our group in the prison yard. Most of the liberated survivors have already left the area, but a couple of stragglers remain. I still wish there were something more that we could do for them.

"It's probably just a mild MCL sprain," I hear Bones say to a woman in muddy jeans and a hooded sweatshirt. The woman has her arm around a young girl in a puffy pink coat, her daughter maybe. The girl looks to be maybe ten or eleven years old, and the older woman leans on her to help keep less weight on her injured knee. "Try to rest and stay off it for a few days once you get somewhere safe."

"I will," the woman says.

"These should help with the pain," Bones says as she drops a handful of pills into the woman's hand.

"Thank you so much," the woman says. The tears pooling beneath her dark eyes glimmer in the moonlight.

I still want to do more for them. It doesn't seem right to send them away like this. I slide a shoulder out of the strap of my pack and reach inside. I pull out the extra magazines and ammo for the rifle, then hold the bag out for the young girl.

"Take it," I tell her. "Should be enough food to last you a few days until you find some place safe."

The girl takes the backpack and slings it over her shoulder. The woman smiles gratefully and then they turn to go.

"Time for us to move, too. We got a long walk home ahead of us," Fletcher says.

"Don't remind me," Army groans.

One at a time, we duck through the hole that we cut in the prison fence. As I wait for the others, I gaze back to look for the woman and her daughter, but they have already vanished into the night.

CHAPTER THREE

After we cross the interstate and make our way toward the dark outlines of the mountains on the western horizon, we see the line of headlights coming in from the north. From half a mile away, we can see the long line of armored vehicles speeding toward the prison across the grassy meadow.

"Here comes the cavalry," I say.

"Pretty big cavalry," Tim says.

We all stare at the glowing lights for a moment in silence.

"You're too late assholes," Fletcher yells at them defiantly.

I can see the smirk on his face, but it disappears quickly when no one appreciates his gloating.

"Let's keep moving," Tim says. "We got a long walk ahead of us."

"Don't remind me," Army groans.

"Army, you are the biggest goddamn baby I ever met in my life," Fletcher says.

We turn our backs to the highway again and continue our trek into the mountains. The big guy mumbles something in Spanish under his breath.

"I heard that," Fletcher warns him by pointing a finger in his direction.

Army waves a dismissive hand and shakes his head.

"Keep talking shit," Fletcher says. "See where that gets you, amigo."

Stitch stops running suddenly, and I nearly stumble over the little mutt in the darkness.

"Shut up," Scout hisses.

Tim stops in his tracks as well and holds up a fist. Stitch lets out a little whimper before he bolts ahead into the darkness.

Twigs snap and I hear a hoarse moan off to my left. My eyes search the dark shapes of the surrounding trees for any signs of the dead. After a couple of seconds, the corpse moves again. It shambles through the brush about fifty yards away. I spot another figure beside it, and several more lurking a little farther behind them. Another one moans just off to my right, and I turn to find several more corpses trudging towards us through the field. The corpses in the surrounding small towns have mostly been cleared by the Reapers, but the gunfire at the prison seems to have drawn out what remains of the dead.

We are still too close to the prison to take them out without the risk of giving away our position. All we can do for now is to make our escape.

"Pick up the pace," Tim whispers as he breaks into a trot.

"Damn it," Army curses softly. "This is as fast as I go."

"Move your ass," Fletcher tells him.

I jog to keep pace with the group. My legs are tired and sore from hiking through the mountains all day, but we just have to suck it up and keep moving.

Last night we took shelter in a deserted ski resort about ten miles away from the prison in Florence. That's where we left all the vehicles. Tim insisted we had a better chance of taking them by surprise if we stayed off the roads in the area completely.

Maybe it was the right call, but I have to question it now that we're out here hiking through the wilderness in the dark with the dead right behind us. It doesn't seem to matter how many of those things we kill. All it takes is a little noise to bring out another wave from the endless tide.

Even as the first group of corpses falls behind us and their moans recede in the distance, countless shapes continue to emerge from the shadows all around us. The clouds above drift to reveal the moon and even more menacing figures closing in around us in the silvery moonlight. It only takes a second for me to calculate from our speed and the distance of the dead that we can't just run away from them. They're closing in on us too fast. We have no choice but to fight.

"Keep running," Tim says when I slow down and reach for my gun. His eyes dart from side to side, then he seems to come to the same conclusion as me. He curses as he brings his carbine to his shoulder and pulls the trigger. A corpse ten feet in front of us drops to the ground. Even with the suppressor, the noise from the gunshot riles up the undead all around us.

I take aim at one of the dark shapes closing from the left and fire several shots. In the darkness, it's hard to tell whether I hit the thing until it falls forward and disappears into the brush.

The others open fire now as we try to push ahead through the undead swarm. I can only hope that we're far enough away from the prison for the gunfire to be heard. The last thing we can afford to do right now is to let that enormous convoy of Reapers know where to find us. I try to glance over my shoulder, but stumble on the rocky terrain. Even if they are coming, getting the hell away from here as fast as possible is the only thing we can do about it.

I can't help thinking that if we'd just taken the vehicles we probably wouldn't be in this situation. I knew it was likely a mistake. In spite of all his training, Tim hasn't had to survive out here like the rest of us. His cabin in the mountains is so secluded that he was pretty much left alone up there through all of this. Still, I know we're better off with him around.

Army begins to lag behind, so I slow my pace slightly and take a few shots at the undead coming from the left side. Army grunts as he shoves a corpse to his right. The rotting thing stumbles into several other shambling bodies and knocks them all to the ground.

Turning back, I discover a corpse a few feet away in the darkness. One side of his face is covered in rotting skin, but the other half of his face appears to have been eaten long ago. An eye dangles from the socket and smacks against the mutilated tissue where his face used to be. The dead man gropes at the darkness. The sudden and horrific sight of the thing makes me pause for a moment. Even after everything that has happened, something like this still can be a shock, at least for me. I raise the rifle; not sure I will have the chance to even get a shot off. I squeeze the trigger, and nothing happens.

Jammed.

"Damn it," I curse.

The thing suddenly falls forward and crashes to the ground. In the moonlight, I glimpse a flash of golden fur and hear a little growl as Stitch darts out of reach of the flailing creature that just tripped over him. He looks up at me and barks loudly as if he is urging me to stop staring at him and get the hell out of there. The stupid dog doesn't notice the arm of the dead thing until it grabs a handful of his scruffy fur.

"Stitch," I yell.

The dog lets out a yelp and tries to run, but the corpse has a firm grip on him. It pulls Stitch closer. The pup growls and nips at the rotting flesh on the dead man's arms, but it does nothing.

I feel someone pulling on my arm and telling me we need to go. The dead are moaning all around us as they close in. All this information registers in my brain, but all I can focus on is what is happening to the stupid dog.

"No!" I yell and shrug my arm loose.

Without even thinking about it, I drop the rifle and rush forward. I kick at the dead man on the ground, then throw myself on top of his decomposing body. The thing lets out a moan. I grab at the putrid flesh on the bicep to break his grip on the whimpering dog. My fingernails dig into the squishy tissue. I raise my arm up and then punch down at the thing with as much force as I can. My knuckles erupt in pain when they crack against the solid bones of the dead man's skull. The corpse falls silent and goes limp on the ground.

Something feels out of place in my hand. I rise to my feet, shaking it stupidly a couple of times as if that will be sufficient to straighten it out.

A massive hand grabs onto my shoulder.

"Come on," Army urges me.

Ignoring the pain in my hand, I turn around. In the darkness, I can barely see the others ahead of us. There are only muzzle flashes in darkness guiding the way. I glance down and notice Stitch trotting beside me. His eyes look up at me as if to check that I'm okay. Normally, I'd never keep pace with him. Either he must be hurt, or he is reluctant to leave my side. Maybe he is afraid. Or maybe he thinks I am.

We finally push through the swarm of the dead. I peek behind me to see that we are starting to pull away from them, but the dead are relentless. Countless corpses trudge through the brush to join the ranks coming for us.

Army starts to fall behind me again. Moonlight glistens off the sweat trickling down his face. He gasps desperately for each breath.

"I knew it," he grunts.

"What?" I say.

"We always end up running," he pants. "I'm so... sick... of running."

"Don't talk," I tell him. "Save your breath."

The dead are still close behind us. While I could definitely run a little faster, I don't want to leave Army behind either. He looks ready to quit. Even in the darkness, I can see it in his eyes. It's a look that I've seen before when a person loses their will to keep fighting.

I notice the others have stopped at a line of trees at the base of the mountain. Muzzles flash in the darkness and then I hear the bullets zipping through the air around us. I hear the grunts and snarls as the rounds pierce the bodies of the dead followed by the sounds of the corpses crashing to the ground in the grass.

We finally catch up to the rest of the group, and Army leans back against the trunk of a tall tree and gasps for air. I look back and see dozens of lurching shapes in the field behind us. Other than a few of the dead that are closest to us, the rest of the corpses have turned back and now trudge toward the prison. There is a fierce battle raging there as well. Headlights shine on figures running in the darkness. I hear the crackle of their weapons firing. At least we know they will be too busy fighting off the dead tonight to come looking for us.

"Hold your fire," Tim says after the last of the dead pursuing us falls still. He lifts his rifle again and watches the prison through the scope for a minute while the rest of us catch our breath.

"We bought ourselves some time," he says. "But not much. We got to keep moving. We got a long walk ahead of us."

Army mutters something in Spanish to himself.

"Quit your crying, Army," Fletcher says. "You can use the exercise anyway."

"Don't even start right now, homie," Army warns him. "I'm not in the mood for your shit."

Fletcher opens his mouth as if to say something else, but then he looks at Army, notices his scowl, and closes his mouth again. One side of his mouth curls into a smirk as he turns and disappears into the shadows of the woods.

CHAPTER FOUR

By the time we hike up the mountainside, dawn is breaking on the eastern horizon. We locate one of the ski lifts, which we follow back up the slope to the abandoned resort. Even though we only left the vehicles here yesterday afternoon, it is still a relief to see them still parked among the abandoned cars in the lot.

As we approach the building, a gust of wind blows the front door open with a long creak of the hinges. We checked the place out yesterday and made sure it was safe, but the sight of the desolate building is not comforting at all.

Our boots scuff against the dirty floors of the lobby and the startled birds nesting in the dusty beams near the ceiling flutter away. The ski resort appears to have been abandoned long before the dead took over. It's already getting harder to tell the difference because the whole world is beginning to look this way now.

We shrug off our gear next to the huge stone fireplace in the middle of the room. Hiking up the mountain was no picnic, but we also were awake all night doing so. Everyone looks exhausted.

I take a quick look around the room. Even though the dusty old furniture is all covered in bird shit, I am so tired that collapsing into the closest cushy armchair seems like a rather good idea. My back aches from hauling my gear up the mountain all night long and my mind is in a daze. I stare at Stitch as he sniffs around on the floor, picks some old bird shit or something off the floor, and chews it.

Stupid dog.

Even though I don't want to move, I reach down and dig out a piece of jerky from my bag. Stitch trots over when he sees me hold it out in my hand and takes it gently with his mouth. He wags his tail as he quickly eats it and then stares up at me with his dark eyes that plead for more. I break off one more piece and hand it over.

"That's it," I tell him. "I don't have anything left for you."

The dog swallows the jerky, licks his lips, and gazes up at me with his hopeful eyes. He knows I'm still holding out on him. I guess I owe him for helping me stay alive last night.

I sigh and hand him the rest of the jerky and he snatches it out of my hand and trots away with it in his mouth. It doesn't matter. I wasn't going to eat it anyway. I can't remember the last time I ate. Even after hiking through the mountains all night, I'm not feeling hungry at all.

Seems like my appetite changed after Cheyenne Mountain fell. It sent me to a dark place and I have been stuck there ever since. Losing Danielle... that had something to do with it, too. She was the only person left that I felt like I really knew anymore. The world just feels like a much more lonely place now.

Don't get me wrong, I'm glad Amanda is still alive. But it's not like she is the same person I remember. I still have no idea what she is thinking most of the time. I'm not so sure that I want to know.

"I don't want to sit around here too long," Tim says.

I look up and see Tim standing next to his brother. Fletcher is crouched down next to Scout on the floor, his arm around her shoulders. She hangs her head as though she lacks the strength to keep it up anymore. Her long dark hair conceals her face as she stares down at the floor.

"Don't, Scout," Fletcher whispers. "We're not giving up. We're going to find him. I promise."

Nothing he says seems to make any difference. I don't see how it could. The odds of us finding Stevie alive... Well, let's just say I wouldn't bet on it. Even if I don't say that out loud, I know it's true. Scout and the others may still be out here just to look for him, but I have my own reasons too.

It's not payback. Not exactly. That is part of it though. I just understand that the Reapers will come for us eventually unless we go after them first. We can't just hide up in the mountains forever and hope they leave us alone. That just isn't the way the world works now.

Fletcher stands up and looks around the lobby as if he is searching for something. His eyes land on Bones and he stares at her while he stalks toward her.

"You said he'd be there," Fletcher says.

"I said he might be," Bones says.

"Yeah," Fletcher nods. "Well, he wasn't there."

"It's not my fault," she says.

"I'm not saying it was," Fletcher shifts his weight from one foot to the other and softens his tone. "But he is still out there, and you must have another idea where to look, right?"

Bones opens her mouth to speak but then stares up from beneath the black bangs of her pixie cut at Fletcher as she considers her next words.

"What?" Fletcher says.

Bones glances at Scout then her eyes drop to the floor for a moment.

"It has to stop," Bones finally says softly.

"What was that?" Fletcher says and leans down closer as if to hear her better.

"You need to face the facts," she says through gritted teeth. "I know nobody wants to hear it, but the little boy that you're looking for is probably..."

Scout lifts her head up suddenly and the two women lock eyes for a moment.

"I know it isn't what you want to hear," Bones tells her. "But running around like this is just going to get more people killed."

She pauses for a moment and takes a deep breath.

"I want to help you," Bones continues. "But not like this. I thought I was finally getting away from all this violence."

"I knew it," Fletcher says. "I knew we couldn't trust her."

"I just want it to stop," Bones raises her voice to keep Fletcher from interrupting her again. "We can't go on like this and keep killing each other until no one is left. It needs to stop."

Tim has made his way across the lobby in that quiet way he has of moving around without being noticed. He places a hand on his brother's shoulder and then pats him gently a couple of times.

"We can finish this conversation back at the cabin, alright?" Tim says. He waits a moment to make sure the conversation is over, and then he gives his older brother one more pat before letting go of his shoulder. "Let's get going."

Fletcher glares at Bones for a long moment before he exhales loudly through his nose and walks away shaking his head. Bones eyes him with an unflinching stony expression. I know this isn't going to be the end of this conversation.

Reluctantly, I grab the armrest on the side of the couch and pull my tired body up from the cushion. I grab my backpack and rifle off the floor.

Everyone else wearily gets up and gathers their gear and then we slowly and wearily trudge out to the vehicles.

A few flakes of snow drift down from the grey clouds that blanket the mountain. Between the exhaustion from a sleepless night and the crisp chill in the air this morning, every movement takes much more effort than it should. The last few months have taken quite a toll on me. Not just physically, but mentally and emotionally.

And it isn't getting any easier. Every day is a fight for survival now, but it feels like there isn't much left worth fighting for.

"We can't afford to make any stops," Tim tells Fletcher as he opens the door to the Jeep. "If this snowstorm lets up, I don't want to be leaving any tracks."

"You don't need to tell me that," Fletcher says as he closes the door of the Jeep and starts the engine.

"I know," Tim says. "Just making sure we're on the same page, Chuck."

"You worry too much," Fletcher smirks.

"See you back at the house," Tim says and gives the door a couple of loud smacks before he heads back to the old pickup.

I climb into the open back of the Jeep behind Fletcher and Scout. Stitch hops into the back beside me and his breath puffs like a steam engine as he pants excitedly about going on a car ride.

Tim gets the rusted old pickup going and then circles around the parking lot and drives toward the winding road down the mountain. Fletcher shifts the engine of the Jeep into drive and follows along behind him.

Once we start moving, Stitch settles beside me and rests his muzzle on my leg. I pet his head and the dog closes his eyes. It puts my mind at ease for a minute.

Fletcher eyes me in the mirror. He has been around me enough now to know when something is bothering me. Even if he isn't saying anything about it, I catch him keeping an eye on me from time to time.

When we get to the highway, Fletcher diverts his attention away from me when Tim hooks a left turn in the pickup truck.

"Didn't we come the other way?" Scout asks Fletcher. "Why did he go left?"

"Not sure," says Fletcher. "Probably trying to steer clear of the prison. Might be he just wants to avoid Pueblo after what happened last time. I'm sure he's got his reasons. Just relax, babe."

"I just hope he knows where he is going," Scout says.

"I won't tell him you said that," Fletcher laughs. "Don't worry. Tim knows these mountains better than anybody."

"We might run out of gas," Scout says.

"Scout," Fletcher sighs. He turns and looks at Scout for a long moment until she turns her head the other way and stares at the mountains in the distance.

"We'll be okay," Fletcher says.

A few miles down the road, we pass a brown sign on the side of the road halfway buried in tall grass and purple wildflowers. San Isabel National Forest is written in faded white lettering and barely visible above the vegetation.

This might not be the fastest way home, but it is much safer. Most survivors avoid these roads through the national parks where there is no fuel or anything else worth scavenging. You get stranded here, several days hike from anything, and you may never make out alive. This area of Colorado is surrounded by miles of dense forests, towering mountains, and even an unlikely five-mile stretch of sand dunes just to the north of our cabin.

Before all of this, this vast wilderness seemed incredibly beautiful. Now it just feels like further proof that the world is really out to kill us all. That's how it feels to me at least. Every day I wake up, I know there is a pretty good chance I might not see the sunset. It is a statistical certainty that death will eventually happen for all of us, but out here there are a lot of ways that it will happen sooner than you think.

The falling snow is now thick and heavy and collects on the ground all around us. By the time we reach the sandy dunes, they are nearly covered in white powder, just like the mountain range along the eastern horizon. A pair of corpses shuffle through the drifts in the distance, leaving trails of trudging footprints in the snow behind them. That's when I look back and notice the tracks in the road behind our vehicles and I just hope we either get enough snowfall to cover them up soon or enough warmth to melt the snow completely.

CHAPTER FIVE

By the time we hike up the mountain, the skies have cleared. The warmth of the midday sun is already melting away the last of the snow. It's a relief. Not just because the tire tracks that we left in the snow are probably gone by now, but it also means we don't have to deal with the inevitable arrival of winter just yet.

Not too long ago, I thought we were the lucky ones. We all beat the odds by managing to survive these last six months. But I am starting to understand the chances of any of us making it to spring aren't particularly good. It's impossible to feel lucky when you're convinced your days are numbered.

We finally reach the mountain cabin late in the afternoon. On the porch, Amanda sits with Stacy, her newborn cradled in her arms. When Stacy notices movement in the trees, she stands up. She hands the baby off to Amanda, and then she reaches for the sniper rifle propped against the frame of the front door. She watches closely until we emerge from the tree line. Tim raises a hand and waves at his wife. Finally, Stacy exhales and sets the rifle down again to retrieve her child from Amanda.

Even though my body is exhausted, I can feel my muscles tense as we approach the house. I look up from the damp earth and see Amanda watching me. Our eyes meet for a moment, then I look down to the ground again. My stomach complains. I can't tell if it is because I still haven't eaten or because something about seeing Amanda still makes me such anxiety that I almost feel ill as a result.

It's not supposed to be like this.

I should be glad she is alive. I *am* glad. That's what I tell myself anyway. Even if it feels like she is a completely different person than the woman I remember.

I can't get used to looking her in the eyes and not recognizing the person I knew. Now she is the woman that lied to me. The woman that got Danielle and a lot of other people killed.

I know it is more complicated than that. Amanda had been through hell. Maybe it will get easier to accept eventually. For now, I just try not to look at her. At least until I figure out how to accept Amanda for who she is now.

"Everyone okay?" Stacy asks.

Tim nods as he steps onto the porch. He drops his gear on the rocking chair and puts an arm around his wife. He squeezes her shoulder affectionately as he leans down slightly to give her a kiss on the top of her head.

"We're okay," Tim assures her.

His eyes go down to the baby, wrapped in a powder blue blanket. Stacy passes his son to him. She looks us over again as we all trudge up to the house.

"There's some soup on the stove," she tells Fletcher.

"Thanks, sis," he says. He opens the front door and steps aside to let Scout and the rest of us go inside.

I linger until everyone other than Amanda has gone inside. She hasn't moved from her chair and the way she is looking at me while holding her hands tensely in her lap, I can tell she wants to tell me something. A sense of obligation makes me feel like I should wait outside with her, even though I get the feeling this will be another unsettling conversation that I am too tired to have right now.

Fletcher looks at me expectantly for a moment. His gaze shifts to Amanda sitting in the other chair on the porch, and then retreats inside and closes the door behind him.

I stand there for a moment and try to think of what to say. Amanda smiles uncomfortably and clears her throat.

"You look... tired," she says.

I know I probably look a lot worse than tired. I'm filthy, malnourished, and depressed. I'm sure I look like hell. But whatever. She is just trying to find a way to get to what she really wants to talk about.

"It was a long couple of nights," I say.

"Did they figure out what happened to the boy?" she asks. "Stevie?"

"He wasn't there," I say.

It feels hard to keep my feet in one place. The awkward conversation is making me uncomfortable. I just want her to say what she needs to say.

She places a hand on her belly. She lowers her eyes and is still for a moment. I swipe at the back of my neck where it feels like an insect is biting me but find there is nothing there anymore. Maybe there never was.

"You feeling okay?" I ask her.

A memory flashes in my mind of waking up to the sound of Amanda coughing and vomiting in the bathroom. That was how I found out she was pregnant. Later on, she confessed she had been afraid to tell me. She was afraid I'd tell her not to keep the baby. It was a thought that crossed my mind. I could barely take care of myself let alone a child.

"It started yesterday," Amanda says. "I can feel her. I feel the baby moving."

She looks up at me and removes her hand from her abdomen as if to let me feel her moving baby, too.

"That's good," I tell her. My hands burrow into the warm pockets of my jeans where I won't have to worry about what to do with them.

"I'm sorry," she says.

"It's okay."

"No," she says. "It isn't okay, but it's not like I can undo any of this."

I stare at her for a moment because that isn't exactly true. But I'm not about to point that out.

"Blake," she says.

"I didn't say anything," I say.

"You didn't have to," she says. "I can tell what you were thinking."

"I wasn't," I insist.

She stares at me for a long moment until it makes me uncomfortable enough that I look away.

"Is that really what you want?" she asks me.

"No," I say.

"Then what?" she says. Tears fill the corners of her eyes.

"I don't know," I say.

"I lost so much," she says. "I know this isn't going to fix the things that happened. I know that. But this baby... I know it won't give us our life back, but at least it might give us some kind of life again. Something worth living for."

I can't help but shake my head at the things she is saying. Talking about this baby like it is ours. As if we are just going to be a happy family again. It all just sounds insane.

"Take a look around, Amanda," I say. "You know what it is like out there. Do you really think this world is any place for a child?"

"We're safe here," she says.

A scoffing laugh comes out of me when I hear her say that.

"Stop laughing at me," Amanda says. She presses her lips together and clenches her fists in her lap.

I compose myself once more by closing my eyes and pinching the bridge of my nose while I consider my next words. I know I'm tired and could say something careless that would turn this into a real argument.

"I'm not trying to make you upset," I tell her.

I wait until she settles back into the chair again.

"You know as well as I do that no place is safe anymore," I say calmly. "I spent the last three days out there looking for a missing kid, even though I know damn well he is probably dead. That's just what happens to kids now, Amanda. It's inevitable. That's just what happens. That's what happened to Abby."

Saying that name makes me lose my train of thought for a moment. It still brings up that last image of her in my mind. The sight of her lifeless eyes staring at me through the chain link fence that surrounded the playground of her school. As much as I wish it would go away, it's always going to be with me.

"Even if that child was mine," I finally manage to say, "I don't think I could handle going through that again."

Amanda just stares at the empty space between us. Her raddled face is pale with horror as her watery eyes gaze at the reality she did not want to accept. I didn't want to have this conversation, but maybe it needed to happen anyway.

Inside the house, the baby cries. The sound makes both of us look at the door to the cabin briefly, though I'm not really sure why. The cries of a baby trigger an instinctual reaction. It's in our nature to try to help them, even when we know we can't.

"I can't just give up," Amanda says. "I don't want to. Stacy—"

"Stacy and Tim have no idea what they're in for," I interrupt her.

Through the front window, I watch Tim take the crying baby from his wife and try to soothe him by bouncing him gently and shushing him.

"They think we can just stock up on supplies, hide up here through the winter, and the whole world will just leave us alone."

It sounds so idyllic and unrealistic. Hearing it out loud makes me roll my eyes.

"This will only last so long," I warn her. "You, of all people, should know that by now. You were there. You saw what happens."

I stop myself from saying more. Even if I do still blame her for the things that happened at Cheyenne Mountain, bringing it up again won't make anything better.

Amanda brings her hands up suddenly and buries her face in her palms.

"Hey, I'm sorry," I tell her.

I knew this conversation would end up like this. I guess it was my fault. Maybe I could have just lied to her and pretended like I thought that everything was going to be okay in the end. Right now, I just don't have it in me.

"Don't listen to me," I shrug. "Nobody really knows what will happen. Just forget I said anything."

I watch her cry silently into her hands for a moment longer. Even though I tried, I can't take back what I said. The damage is done now. I knew it would end up like this.

"Damn it," I mutter to myself.

I turn around and reach for the doorknob.

"Blake," Amanda pleads. "Don't leave. Please."

I look back over my shoulder one more time. Something in her voice reminds me of the woman I remember. I search her glistening eyes for several seconds, but the feeling slips away, and I feel like I'm talking to some stranger.

"I need to sleep," I tell her. "I'm just tired."

"Okay," she says. "Goodnight, Blake." She stares at her bony hands in resignation.

I go inside the cabin, close the door, and head down the hall to find a quiet spot to sleep.

CHAPTER SIX

Early the next morning, before daybreak, I wake up to the sound of Army snoring like a buzzsaw on his bedroll across the room. I sit up in the bed next to Amanda and Stitch picks his head up and grumbles at me for disturbing him. Then he stretches his legs out and falls back asleep.

The cabin only has two bedrooms for eleven people, plus a baby and a dog. It's hardly comfortable. As my eyes adjust to the dark, I see Fletcher with his head propped up on his rucksack, his beat-up cowboy hat covering his face. Scout is tucked in a sleeping bag beside him. The only reason I am fortunate enough to have the bed is because Amanda is pregnant, and no one was going to make her sleep on the floor.

What we really need is another house. Unfortunately, the closest neighboring house is several miles away and nothing like what we have. No power or running water. It's pretty much just a shack.

After we got here, I suggested we search for a bigger house. Maybe a place like that ranch we found with all the supplies and the bunker. The one that burned down. There must still be other places like that out there still. Even though Tim admitted he thought I was right about that, he told me he had no intention of leaving his home.

"Don't worry," he assured me. "We'll make space."

I didn't realize it at the time, but what he meant by that was we would build an addition on the house. That idea would never have occurred to me. It's just not something that I have the knowledge to do. Besides, building anything when the whole goddamn world is ending just seems kind of pointless to me. Tim, on the other hand, built this place. To him, making the place bigger seemed like the most logical solution. So that's the plan.

I finally can't ignore my bladder any longer and get out of bed as quietly as possible. Fletcher picks up his hat for a moment and watches me as I head for the door, then he pulls his hat back down over his eyes.

In the bathroom, I flip on the light. I almost start to unzip my jeans before I notice someone sleeping in the bathtub. Elise grunts and squints her eyes against the sudden brightness. She holds up her arm to block the light.

"Sorry," I mumble and flip the light off again.

I turn to leave and stumble over Stitch. He yips and looks up at me like I'm an idiot for noticing him creeping around behind me in the pitch-black hallway.

Damn this house is too crowded. I need to get out of here.

I open the front door of the house and discover a large figure standing in the darkness of the porch. I start to turn and flee back inside the house before I realize it is just Tim.

"Shit, man," I blurt before I let out a sigh of relief.

"Didn't mean to scare you," he says.

"What are you doing out here in the middle of the night?" I ask him. "Is something wrong?"

Tim hesitates for a moment as though he is considering his answer.

"No," he says. "The baby. He was up crying tonight. Has a little fever or something."

"Did Bones check on him?" I ask.

"Yeah," he says. "She did."

He turns his head, and his eyes search the dark shapes of the trees surrounding the cabin once again.

"Said it could be some respiratory virus or something. He seems okay though, I guess," he adds. "Stacy got him back to sleep about an hour ago."

"So, what are you still doing up?"

"I guess I still got a lot on my mind," he says.

The moment really allows me to see things from his perspective. I remember how overwhelming it was, even before all this. I can't even imagine what he and his wife must be feeling now.

"I guess you would," I say.

A cloud of his warm breath swirls in the crisp night air. He seems like he wants to say something else, but he doesn't know how to say it. I decide it is best not to ask questions. I'll give him a minute to figure it out. Besides, the frigid air is making the urge to piss unbearable any longer.

I step off the porch and walk a few feet in the dark, snapping twigs beneath my feet, until I get to the closest tree. Stitch trots up alongside me and lifts his leg and starts to urinate on the tree as well. The dog stares up at me while he pees.

"Stop it," I tell him. "You're making this weird."

The dog just keeps looking at me until I zip up and walk back to the cabin. Tim doesn't even seem to notice me as he continues to gaze into the black void between the towering trunks of the mountain trees. I pause on the porch and look over at him. The guy clearly has a lot on his mind. I feel like I should say something to put him at ease, but don't know how to go about it.

"Were you afraid?" Tim asks me. He turns his head to look over at me. "When your wife was pregnant... the first time."

"No," I say. "Not really."

He furrows his brow like my answer is making him wonder if he is feeling something unusual.

"I was too young, I guess. Didn't really grasp the situation," I explain. "If I did, I probably would have been a little scared, sure."

Tim presses his lips together and nods slightly, like he appreciates my answer but doesn't feel reassured.

"It's not really the same for you," I say.

One of his eyebrows rises as he stares at me and wonders curiously where I am going with that statement.

"What do you mean?" he asks.

"I didn't have all this going on," I say and lift my arm and wave it around to indicate everything around us. "I knew that everything was going to be okay back then... right up until the day it wasn't anymore. Now, I suppose I'd probably be pretty scared, too."

"But you aren't," he says.

It takes a second for me to realize what he is getting at. Even when it clicks, I continue to stare at him blankly in response because I'm not really sure how I feel about it. The baby still just feels like this thing that is happening to Amanda. I don't think of it as something that impacts me at all.

"I guess our situations are pretty different," Tim finally says. He turns his head away so that his eyes gaze out at the blackness once more.

"So now what?" I say to redirect the conversation to something that bothers me less to think about. "We going to head back out today and keep searching for the kid?"

Tim inhales deeply and thinks the question over in his mind for a moment before he answers.

"No," he sighs.

His response takes me by surprise. I know he doesn't exactly want to be away from his wife and baby, but this probably won't sit well with Scout or Fletcher. I know they aren't just going to give up, even if the odds of us finding Stevie alive again aren't particularly good.

When I don't say anything, Tim makes eye contact with me and nods as though he understands what I am thinking.

"I know what you're thinking," he says.

"They're not going give up," I tell him. "Especially not Scout. Not after everything that's happened. She won't let those bastards have him. No way. If you think they'll just give up and let them win, then you don't know them."

Tim sits down in the rocking chair on the porch and folds his arms across the chest of his flannel shirt, thinking to himself while he nods his head.

"I understand all that," he says. "I've been there before. When you lose something that matters that much to you, it's hard to let it go. So, I'm not going to convince them otherwise. I know that anything I say is just going to be ignored, but I've still got to worry about what I got to lose, too. Bones thinks we should pick up some medicine and supplies for the baby in case this virus gets worse. Vaccines if we can find them. Things that Amanda might need, too. Plus, I didn't stock this place up to support a dozen people all winter. If we don't do something about that, we won't make it."

He stops rocking in the chair and stands up. Tim steps to the edge of the porch leans forward and grips the railing to prop himself up as he stares out into the woods.

"I don't plan on letting that happen," says Tim. He stares, unflinching, into the dark forest before him.

Nothing I say is going to sway this man. I know this because I recognize his rigid stare. It is the same stare I had in Chicago, when I decided to go home to find my wife and daughter, even if it meant going it alone.

Our odds of surviving the winter are not good no matter what we do. Our days are all numbered. I don't even need to figure out the exact probability of that. It's a near certainty that we will all be dead before next spring. The best way to live with that knowledge so far has been to pretend I don't know it.

Maybe it won't be the dead that get us. It might not be fighting with other survivors either. It could be pneumonia. Cold temperatures. Drinking the wrong water. Take your pick. Any number of things can kill us now.

I am pretty sure Tim knows that, too. He just wants to believe that there is something he can do about it.

I guess that's just human nature. People have a tough time accepting the fact that they're going to die as long as they're still alive. It's too easy to pretend you will keep waking up forever.

Tim finally looks at me after a long silence. Even though there is no sign of fear in his eyes, I can sense it inside him. I have felt that same fear before. Some men are more afraid of losing the ones they love than they fear dying.

I don't have it in me to disagree with him. It's not like he'd listen. Besides, maybe I'm wrong. Maybe he is adequately prepared and trained to survive in this world. Hell, it's probably just better to let people believe whatever keeps them going.

"You're ..." I pause try to think of something to say that won't sound like complete bullshit. "You're doing what's best for them. I get that."

"It's what's best for all of us," Tim says. "But I can't do it all alone."

He grimaces and a deep sigh slips out through his gritted teeth.

I still don't really know Tim well, but I feel a lot of sympathy for him right now. Maybe it's too late to put my old life back together, but I can still help him. It probably won't make a difference in the end, but at least it is a reason worth waking up for tomorrow.

"You won't have to," I say. "I probably owe you that much anyway for everything you've done for us. Just tell me what you need me to do."

"We're going to have to go into town," he says.

"Blanca?" I say. "It's already been completely looted. There is nothing left there."

"Not Blanca," Tim says. "Pueblo."

"Jesus," I can't help but scoff at the idea. It's just as crazy as going after Stevie with Fletcher and Scout, I guess.

"I know it's not going to be easy, but it's our best option," he says.

"They're never going to go for this," I tell him. "Not in a million years."

CHAPTER SEVEN

"Not in a million years!" Fletcher hollers.

"I told you," I glance over and Tim and shrug my shoulders slightly.

Tim presses his lips together and leans back against the stone slab kitchen countertops. He picks up his mug of steaming coffee and takes a long sip while Fletcher stares at him.

"You're not serious," Fletcher says. "You can't be serious. You just want to go to Pueblo? It's not like we're just going to swing by the shopping mall and pick up some blouses."

"Are you done?" Tim asks his brother.

Fletcher looks like he has more to say but he bites his lip. Instead, he turns and walks away, flailing his arms and shaking his head in his usual dramatic fashion.

"What about Stevie?" Scout asks.

Scout looks around the room.

A drop of water splatters softly in the kitchen sink. The room is silent for a long moment as I stare at another droplet clinging to the faucet, ready to fall.

"I already told you where else to look for him," Bones says. "But there is no way in hell I'm going back there. I'm sorry, I just can't handle that."

I don't remember hearing Bones mention where else we should look. That was a conversation that must have happened when I wasn't around.

"I know what you mean," says Tim. "You all saw what they do to people."

"Please," Scout begs him.

"Look," says Tim. "I'm not out to be the bad guy here, Scout. If you want to keep looking for him, I'm not going to tell you what to do. All I am saying is we have to face the facts and ensure our own survival."

"Face the facts?" Scout says. "He's just a kid, and he is all alone out there. Those are the facts."

Tim winces like she just slapped him. Making the right choices doesn't mean that someone still won't end up getting hurt because of them.

"What if that was your kid out there, Tim?" says Fletcher. "Would you just give up on him?"

The baby coughs and starts to cry. Tim locks eyes with his wife for a moment while she tries to soothe the baby. Then he hangs his head and stares at the tiles on the kitchen floor.

"Even if you find him and get him back here," Tim finally says. "What good will that do if we don't have what we need to make it through the winter? Did you even stop to think about that?"

The room is blanketed in silence once again. No one has the right answer because there are no more right answers. It's all just compromises. Which dark burden you're willing agree to carry around with you in exchange for your own survival.

"Chuck, my boy is sick. Bones thinks we need to get some medicine and supplies."

"She said it's nothing serious," Chuck says.

"Not yet," Bones says.

"Look, Chuck..." Tim sighs. "You do what you got to do. This is what I'm doing. End of discussion."

"I'm not sure anyone cares what I think," Bones finally says in a calm, measured tone. "But for what it's worth, I think Tim is right."

"Of course, you do," Fletcher scoffs. "I bet you would like nothing more than for us to just leave your friends alone—"

"They're not my friends," Bones says.

"Sure, right..." Fletcher laughs. "Maybe we should have that conversation right now—"

"I agree with Tim, too," I chime in.

Fletcher pauses his rant for a moment and turns his head to look at me.

"You too?" Fletcher says. "You're really on board with this?"

"I don't like it any more than you do," I say. "But we need to look at the big picture."

"The big picture..." Fletcher echoes. He turns his head to look at Amanda where she sits between Elise and Bones at the corner of the kitchen table.

"You didn't think that was the right call when it was Abby," he reminds me. "Remember that?"

"I remember how it turned out," I said.

Amanda muffles a pained cry with the sleeve of her green cable-knit sweater.

"You knew that was a possibility before," he says. "Why not now? What changed?"

"I did," I say.

He stares at me for several long seconds.

"I guess you did," he says without trying to hide the disappointment in his voice.

He glances around the room to gauge how many people are on his side.

"I'm with you," Army tells him. "Maybe we should put it to a vote."

"Hold on," Tim interjects. "Nobody gets a vote. That's not how this is going to work. It's not a democracy."

"So, who decides?" Fletcher says. "You?"

"All of us," Tim says. "You want to keep searching, that's up to you. I won't stop you. Anyone who wants to can come with us and help track down supplies. We have a lot to do if we want to survive the winter."

"I can't believe this," Fletcher says.

Fletcher swipes a hand across his face and then rubs his closed eyes with his thumb and index finger. He folds his arm across his chest and sighs and eyes his brother with a contemptuous stare.

The faucet drips again and this time Tim glances over and then walks over to the sink and grabs the decorative steel knobs and turns the water all the way off.

"It's like that, huh?" Fletcher mutters. "I thought you—"

"It's not like anything," Tim interjects. He brings his cup of coffee to his lips and takes half a sip. Tim makes a face like his coffee doesn't taste right suddenly. He puts the cup down, letting it bang loudly against the counter.

"Damn it, Chuck," he says. "We're not arguing about this. I'm done."

Tim storms out of the kitchen and a moment later the front door slams shut. The room falls silent again. Fletcher looks around the room once more. His eyes finally land on Scout. Her hand is balled into a tense fist and pressed against her lips. She blinks her eyes a few times, trying not to cry.

I hope she doesn't cry again. It seems like someone is always crying about something now. Like that does any good. All it does is make everything seem even worse than it is. I can't handle being around so much misery constantly.

"We don't have time for this shit," Fletcher says. He walks over to the kitchen table and swipes up his worn cowboy hat and places it on his head. "We're wasting daylight."

Army and Scout get up from their seats and leave the kitchen. Fletcher looks around the room again, his eyes settle on me for a long moment. Then he gives me that typical smirk of his to let me know my choice to stay behind isn't going to create a lasting divide among us.

"Listen," I start to say, but he holds up a hand to stop me.

"Save it," Fletcher says. "And quit staring at me like you won't ever see me again. We're going to be fine. We'll be back in a couple of days."

"Take care of yourself, Fletcher," I say.

"You know I will," he grins, then he opens the front door and steps out onto the porch. I know Fletcher can take care of himself. Even when I thought he was dead for sure, he turned up again, alive and well. I can't shake the feeling that maybe he won't be so lucky this time.

A moment later, the front door swings open again and Tim steps across the threshold. He pauses for a moment and watches his brother leave, then holds up a hand to wave goodbye before he shuts the door again.

He just stands there for several seconds, clutching the door handle as though he is unable to let go of it. His body sways slightly and he stares down at his muddy work boots while he collects himself.

"You okay, Tim?" I finally ask.

He slowly lifts his head to look at me. He blinks his eyes a couple times and clears his throat slightly before he speaks.

"Yeah," he says softly. Then he clears his throat again. "Yeah, I'm fine."

He glances back over his shoulder at the door once more and then finally releases the handle and returns to the kitchen. He glances around the room again, searching our faces for something that he doesn't seem to find.

"We need to get moving, too," Tim says. "Pack up enough food and water for three days and as much ammo as you can haul."

"I can help, too," Amanda says. She pushes herself up from her chair and walks across the room.

"I think we can handle it," Tim tells her.

"I'm not useless," Amanda reminds us.

"I know," Tim says. "I didn't say you were."

"I still feel like I should go with you," she says. "It's not right that everyone else should risk their lives while I just sit here."

"We talked about this, Amanda," I tell her. "We can't risk putting you and the baby in that kind of stressful environment. Even Bones said your blood pressure has been higher than it should be."

"I know," she says. "I know."

"I'll meet you outside," I tell Tim, then I walk over to Amanda.

I don't really know what to say so I just stand there for a moment like an idiot while I try to figure it out.

"It's just a couple days," I hear Tim say to his wife. "You will hardly even notice I'm gone."

"I'll definitely notice."

I glance back as Stacy gets up on her tiptoes and gives him a kiss. That only makes me feel even more awkward when I turn back around to look at Amanda. She tries to smile but that just makes it even worse.

"We don't have to do this," she finally says. "You don't need to pretend for me. You don't owe me anything."

It stings to hear her say it so plainly, but it also makes me feel a little better because it's true. I reach over and pick up her delicate hand off the table and hold in mine for a moment.

"I guess I'll just see you when I get back," I say. "Maybe we can talk more then. Figure things out."

"Maybe," she says.

I let go of her hand and leave her sitting alone at the kitchen table. It crosses my mind that something could happen out there. Maybe I won't get the chance to come back here and figure things out. Even so, it doesn't seem like it would matter very much to anyone else at all.

CHAPTER EIGHT

Before the world went to hell, the town of Pueblo had a population of approximately one hundred thousand people. That doesn't seem like a lot compared to a city like Chicago, but still, when all of them are murderous mindless corpses that number seems much larger.

I should try not to think about things like that, but honestly, the things that I should feel grateful for are the things that bother me the most these days.

Maybe this is what they mean by survivor's guilt. But that doesn't seem right since I'm still convinced we're all going to die. It's something different then, I guess. Something new that no one is left to diagnose. End of the fucking world syndrome, I guess. Who knows.

It seems like everyone else feels it, too. We don't talk about it, but it's always lingering just below the surface. I pretended it wasn't there for as long as I could. Now, I just can't do it anymore.

"How far is it?"

Tim scowls at the mirror, staring at me until I feel like an irritating child for even asking.

"About another hour," Tim tells me. "As long as we don't hit any snags along the way."

I can tell he doesn't feel like talking right now. Tim is probably still troubled about Fletcher. Still, I want to know some more details.

"When we get there," I start but before I can finish Tim has removed the folded sheet of notebook paper from the inner pocket of his coat and passes it to me across the sheet. I open it up and read through a long list of supplies. Nails, boards, tools, dry wall, medical supplies, and a whole lot of other stuff we can't possibly fit in the truck.

"Where we going to put all this?" I ask him.

Tim points to the screen on the dashboard.

"Our first stop is this truck rental place," he says. "If it is still there, we can borrow a truck."

"Borrow," Elise smiles. "You mean steal."

Tim glances over at her, his face still as serious and stoic as always.

Bones leans across the seat, and I let her take the list from my hand and have a look at it, too.

"We'll have to look all over town to get everything here," Bones says. "That won't be easy."

"Then we'll get whatever we can," Tim says. "We can always come back, but we're not going back empty-handed."

Tim adjusts his grip on the steering wheel. His hands squeeze the leather so intensely that I can see his knuckles turning white.

"Relax," Elise says. She reaches a hand across the center console and touches her brother-in-law on the shoulder. "We're going to be fine."

Tim is not the kind of guy that can't handle pressure. I haven't seen him like this since I met him, though. He must still be thinking about the conversation with Fletcher earlier. Can't really blame him for that. Still, I hope he can keep it together. We can't possibly do this without him.

Stitch sits up from his spot on the seat between me and Bones and stretches his neck. His eyes follow the shambling figures in golden fields alongside the road. He yawns and then pants anxiously as he continues to stare out the window.

"You should have stayed home like I told you," I say and scratch the top of his head until he calms down and his eyes focus on me instead of the dead. He lets out a little whimper and then lays down in the seat again and I continue to pet him.

We make pretty good time until about ten miles outside of Pueblo. Tim is forced to slow down to navigate the mess of derelict vehicles along the road.

"Keep your eyes peeled," he reminds us, even though each of us is already scanning the surrounding fields for anything out of the ordinary, which is pretty much everything since there are corpses walking around all over the place. Even though the sight of so many corpses here is enough to make us uneasy, at least we can assume that with so many of them in the area, we probably don't need to worry about being ambushed by any other survivors. It is just too dangerous around here for that.

"They're getting awful close," Bones says.

"We should try to speed up some more," I agree.

"I can't speed up," Tim says through clenched teeth. "Not without fucking up the truck."

A corpse bangs on the passenger side door panel. It reaches up and claws at the window, smearing black filth across the glass.

"Tim..." Elise says.

"Okay," Tim gives it a little more gas. "I'm going. Just stay cool. We're fine."

Tim steers the pickup between a couple of corpses and an abandoned school bus. He cuts it a little too close and the front bumper of the bus scrapes against the body of the truck.

"Shit," Tim curses.

"You're good," I tell him. "We're clear."

"Maybe this was a bad idea," Elise says.

"Of course," I agree. "It's a terrible idea."

"Then why did you come?" Bones asks me.

I think about it for a moment before I decide how I should answer.

"Because we don't really have another choice," I say.

The truck is silent again for the moment. Tim keeps pushing forward. The truck jostles us as we rumble over a body.

"We got to get off this road," Bones finally says. "There has to be an easier route."

"You see any shortcuts around here?" Tim says.

"I'm just..." Bones notices his tense eyes staring back at her in the rearview mirror and decides not to push back anymore.

"Looks like it might be clear up ahead," I say to diffuse the situation, even though it really looks just as bad.

"Hang on to something," Tim warns us.

I have enough time to grab the door handle with on hand and Stich with the other before Tim drives off the road to steer around a cluster of smashed cars in the middle. I grab on to the seat as the vehicle pitches to the left. We roll over the brush and small branches clatter against the undercarriage of the car. The tires kick up rocks and a cloud of dust. Then Tim cranks the wheel and accelerates back up the ditch and onto the blacktop again. He weaves between a few more abandoned cars and then takes a breath and leans back slightly in his seat.

I release Stitch again and look around. Most of the corpses I see are behind us now. I think we made it through the worst of it.

Then we hear it. The unmistakable whomping noise of a tire going flat.

"Oh no," Bones says.

"What are we going to do now?" asks Elise.

Tim thinks about it for a moment as the truck slows down. The rim grinds against the pavement.

"Maybe we can just keep driving on it," I suggest.

"We still have forty miles to go," Tim says. "We'd never make it that far. We're going to have to walk."

"Why are we walking? Don't you have a spare?" Bones asks.

"You want to change a tire out here?" Tim responds.

"I just need you to keep them off ten minutes," Bones says.

"Ten minutes?" Tim says. "You sure you can do it that fast?"

Bones nods.

"We're not really talking about this," I say.

"We have to give it a shot," Tim says. "If things go south, we will still bug out before those things can box us in so be ready for that."

Our chances of pulling this off are pretty slim. I'm pretty sure we're all about to die, but it was bound to happen eventually. Might as well be today.

Bones opens the door and hops out before the truck even rolls to a stop. I throw open my door and step out onto the snowy pavement. It doesn't take long for the dead to react to us exiting the stranded vehicle. They start moaning and reaching for us as they drag their feet through the heavy snow.

I raise the rifle at a rotting woman with long, dark hair that is crusted in mud on the shoulder of the highway. An unbuttoned flannel shirt reveals her midsection that has been eaten away. Strands of her innards dangle over the waistband of her filthy jean shorts. Her milky white eyes look towards me, her mouth hangs open as though she is about to speak.

I exhale, sending a white plume of hot breath into the air before I squeeze the trigger. Black bits of rotting tissue speckle the layer of white snow on the ground. Even though I try not to think about it, something about so disgusting splattered across the pristine snow makes it even more disturbing somehow.

I scan the area again and take a breath to settle my nerves. There are several more corpses slowly scrabbling up the ditch on the side of the road, but the others in the clearing beyond are still pretty far off. However, there is a whole goddamn horde behind us. Every one of those things we passed before is still pursuing us. It won't take them very long to get here.

"Let's go," I urge Bones as she grabs the jack out of the truck bed. She pumps the lever and the truck lifts off the ground.

Elise walks toward the trio of corpses coming at us on our side of the road. She makes quick work of them with a single silenced shot from her handgun. Just walks over and pops each one of them in the head execution style.

"Help me cover the back," Tim yells. He posts up next to Bones and begins taking out the dead with one precise shot after another.

"Go on," Elise says. "I'll cover the front."

I work my way to the back of the truck to help hold off the swarm with Tim. I notice my hands trembling slightly again as I raise the rifle up and aim. Maybe it's the cold. Maybe it's nerves. It might be that Stitch is barking nonstop inside the truck like a goddamn idiot. I take a breath again and the shakes go away.

"Someone hand me the damn lug wrench," Bones yells.

She lays down on the snowy pavement and slides her body under the truck. Tim lowers the rifle and fishes the lug wrench out of the truck bed and passes it to Bones. Those few seconds are enough to make it seem like we really won't make it.

The dead are already closing in. There is only about twenty yards of pavement separating us from them now. It seems like every time we drop one to find another one is right behind it. Even with suppressors on the rifles, the noise we are making is going to attract even more of them, too.

"Hurry it up, Bones," Tim says when he pauses to eject the spent mag and swaps it for one of the full ones on his vest which he slaps into the rifle.

"Five minutes," Bones says.

"We don't have five minutes," Tim tells her in between shots.

Bones slides out from under the truck and drags the tire around to the vehicle. There isn't much the rest of us can do to help her.

Time seems to slow down as I shift the rifle and shoot again and again. I don't even really notice

Even with all of us firing nonstop, the dead are still closing the distance. We are also burning through most of our ammunition. We might not have any bullets left if we somehow manage to survive.

I hear the quick patter of Elise firing the submachine gun behind us. There is no time to look back, but as long as I still hear her shooting, I know our backs are covered.

I fire the last round from the assault rifle and then reach for handgun in my waistband.

"We're out of time, Bones," Tim says. "Everybody, let's move."

"No, wait!" Bones grimaces as she cranks the lug wrench around. "I got it. Get in the truck."

The dead are right on us now. I take one last shot to drop a dead guy that is barely an arm's length away before I turn and run back to the truck. Bones finishes tightening the final lug nut then turns and uses it on a corpse shuffling over from the side of the road before she hops back in the truck. Stitch is still barking his head off when I open the door and push him out of my seat so I can climb in. I really have to pull myself up to get in the truck again. Then I realize why it seems higher off the ground.

"The jack," I say.

"Close the fucking door!" Tim yells as he fires up the ignition.

I reach for the handle to close the door, but it's too late. One of the dead bastards reaches into the car. I cling to the door handle to try and keep it from squeezing all the way inside. The tires on the other side of the truck spin in the snow when Tim punches the gas. Finally, they find traction and pull the truck forward enough to topple the jack. As the tires on our side hit the pavement again, I lose my grip on the door handle.

The dead guy hanging on to the door lunges at me and snaps his jaws on the air as I pull my arm away. Stitch growls and attacks the thing. The dog sinks his teeth into the pale flailing arm of the corpse and distracts him long enough for me to lift the gun up and shoot him in the head. The body falls and tumbles along the pavement as we speed down the highway.

CHAPTER NINE

We might still be alive. We might even make it to Pueblo. Still, we're hardly out of the woods. I reload our empty magazines with the last of our ammunition.

"Only enough rounds to fill four magazines," I tell Tim as I pass him two of the cartridges.

"We won't have enough bullets to shoot ourselves out of another situation like that," Tim says.

"So, I guess we better make sure we don't have another situation like that," I say.

Tim glances up at the mirror and stares at me for a moment.

"We should be able to pick up some more ammunition in Pueblo," he says. "We don't need to panic."

I didn't really mean to imply anything negative by that, but he seems to think I might have.

"I'm just saying we need to be careful," I add.

Tim returns his eyes to the road.

"That sounds good to me," Bones chimes in and she wipes the grease off her hands with a rag. "I've had enough excitement for one day, I think."

"You did good back there," I tell her.

"Not a big deal really," she says. She stops cleaning her hands for a moment and looks up. I notice a smudge of black grime on her face. I make a gesture toward my own cheek with my hand, and she understands and wipes her face with the rag. "I've been in worse spots than that. More times than I care to remember."

She finishes wiping her hands clean and then tosses the rag back into her backpack.

"At least this time, everyone came out of it alive," she says and forces a smile.

Stitch sees her smiling and his tail starts to wag. He inches closer to Bones and licks her cheek. She smiles and laughs genuinely then as she pets his scruffy neck.

"Such a sweet boy," Bones tells him.

He keeps wagging her tail and licking her all over her face until the truck swerves and he nearly falls off the seat. Bones quickly grabs hold of him and hugs the dog close to her.

"I got you, little guy," she tells the dog and then he starts wagging his tail and lifts up his paw until she holds it in her hand. He glances back at me over his shoulder.

"I think he likes you," I tell Bones.

"I like him too. He probably senses that," she says. "Animals are better at reading people than most people are. At first, I only decided to trust you because he does."

"Really?" I ask her.

"Most people would not have taken care of a little dog like this," she says. "They would have eaten him instead of feeding him."

"I've thought about it a few times," I grin.

Stitch looks back at me when I say that as if he understands somehow.

"I'm just kidding," I say and pat Stitch on the head.

"Damn it," Tim curses and slows the truck to a stop.

I look up ahead and see a bridge that is blocked by dozens of abandoned cars. There is no way we can drive all the way across.

"That's just fucking great," Tim sighs as he shifts the car in park.

"What are we going to do now?" Elise asks.

"We can circle back," I suggest. "There has to be another route we can take."

"What makes you think any other way will be any easier?" Tim asks. "Besides, we don't have enough gas to drive all over the place."

"Maybe we can push some of the cars out of the way," Elise says.

Tim considers this for a moment as he scans the area. There are a few dozen corpses walking around on the bridge. Plenty more are scattered in the vicinity and are already shambling toward our vehicle through the layer of snow covering the ground.

"I know we just risked our asses to fix this truck, but I'm not sure I'm feeling quite that lucky," I say.

"Me either," Bones agrees.

"Well, whatever we're doing we better decide quick," Elise says.

"Alright. It's only about five more miles to Pueblo," Tim says while he shuts off the truck and removes the key from ignition. "We can make that hike before dark if we hustle."

"This day just keeps getting better," sighs Elise. She grabs her knitted beanie off the dash and pulls it back over her auburn hair.

"I never said it was going to be a picnic," says Tim. He pops the handle and pushes the door open. The hinge makes a noisy creak as cold air comes rushing into the interior. "Let's move."

We exit the truck, snowflakes pattering our faces from the icy breeze. The dead are already closing in, so we don't even bother shutting the doors before we hurry toward the bridge. Stitch hesitates to jump down from the backseat. He shivers and stares out at the swirling snow and the dead and growls. I have to whistle to get his attention.

"Come on, you idiot," I tell him as he runs to catch up.

It doesn't take long for the frigid air to invade my worn boots. First, the bones of my hands and my feet ache from the cold. Then my fingers and toes start to go numb. Even though we keep jogging to avoid the dead, I'm still so cold. I'm not sure if the temperature is actually dropping or if it just feels like it is the longer we stay out here, but it makes me think that we have yet another thing to worry about. There is no telling how cold it might get tonight.

It's not like we're likely to find a place with electricity and a furnace. We can probably use a fire to keep warm, but any other survivors might see the fire and smoke. They might smell it. They might decide to track us down and see what we have. Survivors aren't all we have to worry about. Maybe the dead will be drawn to the fire as well. I don't really know what might happen. But I don't think I want to find out.

The snow flurries begin to swirl in the blustery wind. Gusts of freezing snow blast against my face. It stings like hell after a while. It makes it hard to see. Luckily, it seems to be just as difficult for the dead. Most of them don't even seem to notice us walking on the shoulder of the road. I guess we at least got that going for us.

Finally, we get close enough to make out some buildings in the distance as night approaches.

"Almost there," Tim yells to be heard over the howling wind. "The temperature is dropping fast. Let's pick up the pace."

That's the last thing I want to do right now. But he is right. We don't want to be running around in the dark and we also need to get out of the storm. I quit thinking about being back inside the warm cabin next to a crackling fire. Time to suck it up and get moving to keep up with Tim and Elise.

I glance over at Bones running along beside me to make sure she is doing okay. Her cheeks are burning red and her lips are turning a pale blue.

"We probably should have checked the weather before we left," I joke.

"That's not funny," she says while holding back a smile.

We pass by a stone sign on the side of the road. The words are mostly concealed beneath a layer of snow that clings to the surface, but I can still see the word 'PUEBLO' clearly enough. Knowing we made it here makes it easier to forget about how cold and miserable I am for a moment. Stitch pauses in front of the entrance to a cemetery on the edge of town. He turns his head to check on us and then watches the corpses wandering further down the road, holding up his back leg awkwardly to avoid touching the cold snow for a moment. As soon as we catch up to him, the little dog runs up ahead of us again.

The grey sky of ironclad clouds darkens toward night. The muted moonlight reflecting off the snow on the ground casts a soft, silvery-blue light. We pass a few small side streets with nothing but darkened houses and a handful of dark figures lurking in the snow. I glance down and notice that most of the snow on this stretch of road is still completely untouched. There are a few footprints here and there, but not that many. Maybe this won't be so bad, I think. Then I regret it immediately. Whenever I start to believe things will be okay, things tend to go south real fast. At least, that's how it seems.

"Damn it," Tim curses.

I get a sinking feeling in my gut.

"What is it?" Elise says.

"That's the place over there," Tim points up ahead to some buildings surrounded by tall wrought iron fencing. As we approach the barrier, I can see what Tim already realized. The place is in ruins. Most of the doors to storage units are open and ransacked. A pair of corpses wander in a parking lot where all sorts of useless belongings (mattresses, rusty lawn mowers, strollers) sit beneath a layer of snow. There is not a rental truck in sight. It looks some survivors might have been holed up when this all started. Probably thought the fences could keep them safe. When that didn't last, maybe they took off in the trucks. Something like that.

"Well, that's a disappointment," says Elise.

I turn around and look up and down the road. With the snow swirling around, I can't see very far at all. The dead that I can see have taken notice of us and are moving stiffly in our direction. The cold or the snow seems to slow them down. Not much, but just enough to be noticeable. Stitch lets out a little whimper and then stares up at me anxiously. He knows it is time for us to move.

"We have to get off the streets," I say.

Tim releases his grip on the iron bars of the fence and turns around. He takes a few seconds to collect his thoughts and then continues walking down the road.

"Where are we going?" Bones asks him.

"This way," Tim tells us.

Bones and I look at each other for a moment. I can tell she is feeling a little uncertain about this as well. It's a little late to turn back now, though. I just hope Tim knows what he is getting us into here.

At the next intersection, Tim pauses and looks up and down the block. I check the ground again and see more signs of the dead dragging their feet through the snow recently. There are definitely a few more tracks here than there was a mile back. I shield my eyes from the falling flurries and scan the road ahead. I can't see much aside from a bunch of abandoned cars, some darkened structures, and some figures moving in the street.

"We can probably get inside one of these houses," Elise gestures down the side street to our right.

"No," Tim says. "It's just up the block."

"What is?" Bones asks him.

"The goddamn store," Tim snaps. "Come on."

We make our way down the next block, weaving through the cars in the road. Now there are lots of tracks on the snow. The dead notice our presence as we approach and begin to moan and reach for us as we run by them. We can't afford to start shooting now. Not here. This place belongs to the dead. A single gunshot would probably draw hundreds of the dead from the surrounding area. Even if I can't see them in the snow, we can tell they are out there.

Tim slides to a stop after we circle around an overturned ambulance just ahead of the next intersection.

"Hold up," he tells us, raising a fist next to his head, in case we couldn't hear him over the wind.

Up ahead I can see the remains of the sign for the store that Tim was hoping to reach. The entrance looks to be surrounded by the dead. The building is gone. From here I can't tell if it burned down or what, but all that remains is a few bits of wall protruding from the rubble.

This isn't our night at all.

"No," Tim mumbles as he stares at the ruins in disbelief.

"Watch it," Elise says. She sidesteps and raises her handgun and fires at a corpse coming up behind Tim. The corpse groans and collapses to the ground, spilling black gore all over the snow.

"Shit," Tim curses.

"I had to," Elise says.

"I know," Tim says. He glances around the street again. The dead all heard the shot. Dozens of them are coming down the road in each direction. They're all moaning and heading toward the intersection now.

"Tim..." I say.

"Over there," Tim points down the side street to an alley in between a pair of older brick buildings. Some kind of store. It doesn't matter. We just need to get the hell out of sight. In the alley, Tim tries to open the back door for a salon. He curses when it's locked then moves to the door of the building on the opposite side of the alley. It swings open when he pulls the handle. Tim stares into the dark interior for a moment, apparently in shock that the place is unlocked. Then he raises his handgun and disappears inside. While Elise and Bones rush in behind Tim, I take a quick look back up the alley and see the dead coming up the passage behind us. I'm not really sure going inside is a good idea, but we don't have a lot of other options.

"Damn it," I curse under my breath before I go inside. When I shut the door, everything goes black in the windowless stock room. My hands find the deadbolt and as soon as I lock us inside, the dead start banging on the other side of the door.

CHAPTER TEN

There is a wall of darkness all around me. We silently listen for any sounds coming from inside the building, but all I can hear are the dead pounding relentlessly at the door behind me. I can't see anything, but this place smells of dust and mildew. There are definitely worse smells. There is a click in the darkness and then a beam of light appears. Tim sweeps the flashlight around the windowless room. There are boxes piled all over the place and shelves overloaded with stacks and stacks of books.

"This is a bookstore," Bones says.

It's one of those painfully obvious observations people feel the need to make for absolutely no reason sometimes.

"No shit," Elise says.

"Keep it down," Tim reminds them. "We might not be alone."

The flashlight beam settles on a door across the room that likely goes to the sales floor. We make our way to it through the boxes and then wait for a moment while Tim opens the door a crack and peeks through it. Once he takes a look around, he lets out a long breath and pushes the door open all the way.

Just enough moonlight spills through the front windows of the store to illuminate the empty aisles between the shelves of countless books. It's not a very large shop, but there are books everywhere. The place appears to be completely untouched, too. It's like no one has set foot inside of here since this all began.

Tim lowers his pistol and holsters it.

"Seems safe to assume we're alone in here," Tim says. He sweeps a hand over a layer of dust on the display table beside him. Then he examines his gloves and wipes them off on his pants.

I wander over to a small cafe in the back of the store and stand there for a moment and stare down the aisle at the dead shambling by the front windows of the store. My warm breath hangs like a cloud in front of my face in the calm, frozen air. I don't know how long it will last, but for the moment we are safe enough to catch our breath here. I take down a chair that is positioned upside down on a small dining table and set it on the floor.

Stitch whines softly. I look down to see him shivering as he stares at the windows too. Clumps of ice cling to his scruffy fur. I bend down and shrug my shoulders out of the straps of my backpack and set it on the ground against the display case of the coffee bar. The food inside it is shriveled and covered in mold. I locate an old towel on the counter and I pick it up and use it to dry Stitch off as much as I can. He looks up at me and gives me an appreciative wag of his tail.

"I can't believe this place," Bones says. She picks up a book from the shelf and flips through the pages. "It's looks like nothing ever happened."

"Guess nobody wanted a bunch of lame boring books," Elise says. She looks down at the pictures on the dusty covers with obvious disinterest.

"We can shelter here for the night. Since we're in here, take a look around. We might be able to use some of these," Tim says. "Medical books. Engineering books. Natural remedies. Shit like that. Anything we might need to know."

"I already know everything," Elise grins.

Tim eyes her for a long moment, then a subtle smile appears on his face. He sets his gear down on the floor and snatches the beanie off her head.

"Not hard to tell you're related to my wife," Tim tells her. He shakes the snow off her cap and hands it back to her.

"I'll be sure to let her know you said that," Elise says.

"I hope you do," Tim says. "That'll mean we make it back home first and that's all I give a damn about right now."

The dead continue to hammer and claw at the back door. Tim stares over his shoulder at the sounds coming from the back room.

"Sounds like there are more of them out there now," he says.

"The door will hold," I assure him. "It's steel."

He nods his head slightly, but he is still squinting slightly like he isn't sure he believes me. Tim might have a lot more training than all of us, but he has had the luxury of being away from all of this in the mountains.

"I know," he tells me. "It's just those sounds they make."

"Gets under your skin," I say.

"Yeah," he says.

"You get use to it," I tell him. "Sort of."

I say this to assure him even though I don't think I'll ever really get used to it myself. I give him a reassuring pat on the shoulder, but he just returns a sidelong stare that makes me immediately regret it.

"Was that supposed to make me feel better or something?" Tim asks me.

"Well, yeah, I guess."

"It didn't," Tim informs me.

"I'll go check the cafe," I say. "See what I can find."

"You do that," Tim says.

I guess I kind of thought after our talk this morning and agreeing to come along that Tim might have started to see me as a friend. Maybe something I did pissed him off. It could just be the way he is out here. I don't really know him well enough to know. But it's probably better to leave it alone.

There isn't much behind the counter of the cafe. There is a small fridge and freezer that I know better than to open. None of us will want to smell whatever rotten food is in there for the rest of the night. I do manage to locate a few boxes of protein bars and a dozen three pound bags of coffee. There are boxes of sugar packets and powdered creamer that I grab as well. That would have been enough to make my day a month ago, but that's not going to do much to keep us alive for the winter.

After I pack the stuff into our bags, I open up one of the protein bars and eat it while I wander around and look around the bookshelves for anything useful. Then I stop chewing the protein bar in my mouth when my eyes land on something familiar. On the shelf in front of me there a copy of the book I wrote years ago. It seems like a something from another lifetime.

I shove the rest of the protein bar in my mouth before I reach out and pick up the copy. The dust shakes free of the smooth matte cover. The sight of it brings back a flood of memories from my old life. It reminds me of all the things I've lost that I will probably never come to terms with.

"Find anything good?" Bones says.

I hear her voice, but I'm still so lost in thought that I'm not aware that she is talking to me.

"Blake," she says.

I take in a breath suddenly and turn to look at her. It takes my eyes a second to focus on her face, but when they finally do I notice she is looking down at the book in my hands. I clear my throat and set the back on the shelf.

"Nothing yet," I say.

I kind of hope she doesn't decide to start asking questions right now. Maybe she didn't notice anything about the book or that I'm acting strange right now. Then she reaches for the book and picks it up.

I hadn't mentioned much about my life to her or anyone else that is still alive for that matter. Amanda knows obviously. Fletcher. But the more time passes, the less I tend to talk about the past. She turns the book over and looks at the back over. Her eyes land on the picture and then she lifts her head and looks me in the eyes again.

"You wrote this?" she asks me.

I just sort of shrug and nod my head.

"That's you?" Bones points her finger at my photo on the back.

"It was a long time ago," I say.

She opens up the book and starts to flip through the pages. I take it out of her hands before she flips the title page and put it back on the shelf.

"Do me a favor," I say. "Don't make a big deal out of it. Pretend you never saw it."

I turn and start to walk away down the aisle of books.

"You're just going to leave it here?" she says.

"Yeah," I tell her.

"Don't you want to hang on to a copy of it?" Bones asks me.

I stop and turn back around. She holds the book in her hands again.

"For what?" I say. "It's not like anything in there is useful to us now. Nothing in there will ever matter to anyone again."

"I'm sorry," she says softly. "I didn't mean to—"

"Forget it," I sigh. "Just forget you ever saw that, okay?"

"I just thought maybe Amanda might like it. You know, to give it to the kid someday," she says. "Something like that."

"It's not my kid," I remind her.

"Listen—" she says.

"My daughter is dead. The less things I have around to remind me of that ever again the better!"

I glance over to the tables in the cafe and see Elise and Tim staring at me. I realize I let my voice get a little louder than I should have. We don't need to remind those things banging on the back door that we're still inside here.

Bones stands there with her mouth open and seems like she is about to try and apologize or say something else that will probably just make things worse. I wish she would have just left it alone like I said.

"Damn it," I curse under my breath before I turn and head for the dark storage room at the back of the store.

I find a stack of boxes to sit down and get myself under control again. I know I overreacted out there. Part of the reason I agreed to come out here was to forget about Amanda and all the things we lost for a few days. It seems like that just isn't possible. You just can't pretend not to feel the pain of all the things you lost. It doesn't work that way. There is no hiding from it. Loss will always find you.

CHAPTER ELEVEN

The cold awakens me before dawn. I have no idea what time it is. I lift my hand to look for a watch, but then I remember I haven't had a working watch for some time.

The dead are no longer pummeling the back door of the bookstore. Something must have lured them away during the night or they eventually wandered off. I get up and stretch out the creaking aches from sleeping on a pile of boxes.

In the front of the store, I see Bones and Elise sleeping on the floor. Tim is still awake. He is sitting in a wooden chair from the cafe in the middle aisle of the store. His hand rests on the rifle laid across his lap. He turns his head when he notices me moving out of the corner of his eye. His right-hand slides toward the trigger slightly, then his tired eyes realize it is just me and Tim relaxes again and returns to watching the dead wander outside the front window of the store.

I make my way over to him and lean against a bookshelf. He sighs loud and deeply enough that I can tell he would rather be left alone. So, I just stare at the store windows for a few minutes and leave him. When his head lolls slightly forward I look back over to see his eyes snap open. His eyes scan around the room for a moment while he tries to figure out how long he had them closed.

I know what he's thinking because I've been there many times before. It used to be so hard to sleep. It was terrifying. Now, I kind of enjoy it again. Especially since I stopped dreaming. It's the only time all of this goes away.

Tim covers his mouth and yawns silently.

"I'll stay up," I tell him. "Keep an eye on things. Get some sleep."

"I'm fine," he says.

I'm not really surprised. These ex-military guys all like to think they don't need sleep. He can't keep this up forever out here though.

"It's almost dawn," I tell him. "Just an hour."

He doesn't answer me. His eyes return to staring out the windows again.

"It'll be fine," I assure him.

"You get your head right again?" he asks me.

"What?" I say.

"Last night," he reminds me. "I need to know if I'm going to have to babysit you out here."

"No," I say. "That was just... I'm fine."

Tim studies my face for a long moment before he seems satisfied and nods slightly.

"Alright," he says.

Then he yawns again and closes his eyes.

I turn my head and continue watching the dead wander aimlessly around the street outside. I try not to think about anything, but that only seems possible when you're not trying. Instead, a memory from years ago surfaces. When she was five, my daughter went through this phase where she had nightmares almost every night. They terrified her so much that she'd wake up screaming. This one night she was so scared she couldn't fall back asleep. She climbed into our bed and tossed and turned endlessly beside me. Finally, I decided to ask her what happened in her dream.

"There were monsters," she said. "They wanted to take me away."

"Monsters," I said.

I can still almost remember the feeling of her arms clinging to me, her face burrowing into my chest.

"It's just a dream, sweetie," I told her.

"It felt real," she said.

"There's no such thing as monsters," I said. "And I'd never let anything take you away from me."

"But daddy," Abby said.

"Just go back to sleep, Abby," I pleaded. "There's nothing to worry about."

At the time, all I cared about was getting back to sleep. It was easy to tell her not to worry because I believed what I was saying. As it turns out, there was a lot more to be afraid of than I realized back then. She was right to be afraid. The monsters did take her away and there was nothing I could do to stop it.

"I'm sorry, Abby," I say.

"What?" Tim says and blinks his eyes several times as he wakes up.

I wasn't even sure I said that out loud. Damn, he's a light sleeper.

"Did you say something?" he says.

"Nothing," I stammer. I turn and "Just... it's sunrise. Almost."

Tim gets up from his chair. He yawns and stretches his arms.

"Thanks for looking out," he says. Tim stares at the windows in the front of the store while he slings his rifle over his shoulder.

The street out front is quiet now. Only a lone corpse wanders down the road.

"We should move now," I tell Tim.

"I'll go wake up those two," Tim gestures to the girls sleeping on the floor near the coffee shop. He picks up his bag and searches around for something inside as he walks out of the room.

I hear a splashing sound and look down the aisle to see Stitch staring at me with his leg up while he pisses on a rack of romance novels. I reach down and pull a bag of peanuts from my bag. He trots over and stares up at me expectantly until I toss a nut and watch him snatch it out of the air with his mouth.

Five minutes later, the front door of the bookstore swings open and we step out into the trampled snow. It looks like there is about five or six inches of snow on the ground, but it's hard to tell for sure after the dead kicked it all around and compacted it underneath their feet. The pristine white surface is muddied here and there with droplets of black coagulated fluids.

"This way," Tim points to the left. We head down the road into the blinding morning sunshine.

Even though the snowstorm is gone, and the skies are clear for now, the air is still cold enough to see our breath and to keep the snow from melting on the ground. If we are lucky this will be one of those strange Colorado days where the temperature climbs forty or fifty degrees in the afternoon. If not, we might have a tough time driving through the mountains. It's not like any plows will be out there clearing the snow off the roads so we can make it home.

On the bright side, the snow isn't just slowing us down. As we make our way down the block, the few corpses that we pass struggle in the snow. They plod slowly through the deeper snow and slide around on the slick, trampled spots. One of the poor bastards crashes to the ground as it desperately tries to reach us. Considering we don't have nearly enough rounds of ammunition left to fight them off, I suppose the snow might be more of a blessing than a curse.

At the next intersection, Tim stops for a moment and looks up and down the cross street. There is nothing but houses in both directions. Stitch stops to wait for us and sniffs around at the trampled ground uncertainly. He looks back at us and waits until he can tell which way we are going and then he continues running down the same road to the next stop sign.

"You sure you know where we're going?" Elise asks him.

"Yeah," Tim says. "Sort of."

"Sort of?"

"I know what general direction we need to go," he says. "Relax."

We pass by a small church and take a left at the next intersection down a small residential street of mostly small single-story homes. I can tell by the lack of tracks in the snow that there hasn't been much foot traffic coming through this way overnight. That's a good sign, I guess.

Tim takes another right when we reach a stoplight. There is a school at the corner that looks like it was used as a shelter back in the early days. Bullet riddled military vehicles still sit in the parking lot behind trampled fences and piles of sandbags. That tattered remains of tents flutter on the ground. The torso of a half-eaten soldier still lies against the tire of one of the trucks. It raises an arm when it sees us in the road.

I don't even want to think about everything that might have happened there. Just the sight of the building reminds me of the night I found Abby.

"It's just up ahead," Tim pants. "See?"

Then I spot the blue sign of the hardware store along the right side of the road before the next intersection. I can also just barely see the top of the building over the roofs of the houses behind the store.

"It's still there," Tim says. "Thank God."

It's a good sign, but I know better than to get my hopes up by now. Something always seems to go wrong whenever I do.

The dead swarm toward the intersection from every direction. Some of the closest ones start to notice us and begin trudging towards through the drifts of snow.

"They spotted us," says Elise.

"Shit," Tim curses.

A tall wooden fence stands between the row of houses and the back of the hardware store. There is a big alley and employee parking lot with several garage-style loading doors. I can't tell for sure, but it looks like one of them might be open.

"This way!" I urge them as I veer off the street and cut to the right toward the receiving dock.

The back of the building is clear except for a pair of stiffs in jean jackets with the sleeves cut off and biker patches stitched all over. The two of them shamble listlessly near the open loading bay door until they hear our boots crunching the snow.

Tim rushes the taller of the two men and raises the rifle to his shoulder to crack the guy in the face with the stock. He loses his footing and only manages to connect with a glancing blow before he tumbles to the ground. The biker collapses on top of him.

That is when I notice the other biker is coming straight at me. Even though his companion was a little taller, this guy was hardly small. I take a couple steps back as he lumbers toward me. My hand reaches for the grip of the gun tucked into my jeans, but I really don't want to have to shoot. Enough of those things already know we are here. We don't need to alert any more of them.

Instead, I lift my boot and try to kick him in the midsection. Maybe I can get him to lose his balance. That turns out to be pretty ineffective. The dead biker wobbles and takes a couple steps back before coming at me again.

Stitch darts at the ankle of the guy. He buys me a few seconds by biting his jeans and tugging them.

That's when I hear the gunshot. The other dead biker collapses on top of Tim and I catch a glimpse of Elise holding the gun in her hand.

No point in messing around with this other one any longer. I pull out my gun and whip it around as the biker lunges for me. Even I'm a good shot from point-blank range. I squeeze the trigger and then his head snaps back. His knees buckle. He collapses near my feet in the snow.

"Come on!" I hear Bones yell.

I stop staring at the dead man on the ground and look up to see Tim shoving away the other corpse that was on top of him. Bones and Elise are already climbing onto the concrete platform to get into the building.

"They're coming!" Bones says and points her finger up the alley.

I peek down the alley and see what has them so panicked. The dead are already closing in on us. Hundreds of them pour into the alley from the street.

Stitch runs toward the loading dock and jumps and barks desperately as Tim climbs up awkwardly onto the snowy ledge. I step over the body of the dead biker and run for the doors. I scoop Stitch up off the ground and set him on the platform. When I try to jump and pull myself up, all the extra weight of my pack makes it impossible to get very far off the ground. I also can't get a decent grip in the snow.

The dead are closing in. The nearest one hobbles by the body of the biker on the ground.

"Help me!" I yell.

I should have tossed my backpack and rifle up there. It's too late now. In the few seconds it will take to do will be too long. The dead will reach me and tear me to shreds.

Damn it. I shouldn't have taken all those bags of coffee. What a stupid thing to die over.

I try one last jump even though I know I can't possibly make it up there on my own. Tim grabs my backpack and pulls until he slips in the snow. It's just enough though. I get myself halfway onto the ledge, and Bones and Elise join him to pull me the rest of the way up. I scramble across the ground to get a few feet away from the edge as the dead reach the platform. It doesn't seem like they can pull themselves up four and a half feet onto the ledge, but I watch as they reach for us and claw at the concrete and moan until Tim grabs a strap dangling from the bottom of the overhead door and pulls it down on their limbs. He lifts it enough to let them free their arms and then slams it back down several times until the door is completely closed and we're gasping to catch our breath in the dark.

CHAPTER TWELVE

We made it. Even if it seems like we might not ever make it back out alive. The dead outside the loading bay moan and bang their fists on the metal door. The rumbling sound echoes in the cavernous and pitch-black interior of the hardware stare.

Something clicks in the darkness and then a bright light flashes right in my eyes. I look away and raise my hand to block it out.

"Sorry," Elise says. She moves the light out of my eyes and sweeps it around the interior of the warehouse. There are towering shelving units that nearly touch the roof. They are loaded with boxes and pallets of merchandise.

Elise moves the light around the room until it passes over a dark crimson spot on the paved floor.

Dried blood.

Beside the blood is a pile of rotting flesh that still somewhat resembles a person who was devoured a long time ago. Can't even tell if it was a man or a woman now. The right side of the head was eaten clean down to the bone. Strands of intestines and half-eaten organs lay in a pile on the floor. The only thing that remains below the waist are some bones and sinew and a pair of blood-covered jeans. Stitch walks near the mess and curiously sniffs it then retreats with his tail between his legs.

"That's fucking gross," Elise says.

"Quiet," Tim whispers. "Listen."

We stand there for a moment in silence while Elise continues to scour the dark room with the flashlight. I'm not exactly sure what we are supposed to be listening for since all I can hear is the sound of the dead relentlessly assaulting the loading bay door. All I see is boxes everywhere.

"I thought I heard something," Tim says. "Something inside. Give me that."

He takes the flashlight from Elise and holds it up beside his pistol before he walks toward the rows of shelves. I take out my gun to have it ready and then we move slowly through the warehouse. Tim pauses at each corner to check up and down each aisle. They're all empty except for a few handcarts and unloaded pallets.

Then we reach the swinging door to the sales floor. Tim shines the flashlight through the window in the store and then quietly pushes the door open. The front of the store is nearly as dark as the back. The faint light coming through the windows at the front entrance provides just enough illumination for us to avoid falling over in the dark. There is plenty to trip over as well. The aisles still seem to be fairly well stocked but are in a state of disarray. There are lots of opened boxes and items left on the floor of the aisle. Looters definitely discovered this place before us, but they still left plenty behind. Maybe something got them before they could leave.

Now that we are away from the back doors, it's easier to hear the sounds inside the store. We certainly aren't all alone here. Tim stops moving when something inside the building crashes to the ground. Then we hear a moan responding to the sound from off to our left. Another guttural noise comes from the opposite side of the store as well.

Tim pauses when the aisle comes to an intersection and crouches down on the ground and pokes his head out to peek around the corner. He holsters his sidearm and switches to his rifle and silently checks it quickly.

I get the feeling this could be worse than we realize. We don't even know if the front entrance is secure. The doors could be wide open. For all we know there could fifty of those things in here.

I tuck my handgun away and ready the assault rifle as well.

"Stick together, no matter what," Tim whispers. "We good?"

He waits until each of us acknowledges him with a nod before he turns back toward the aisle. Then he stands up and pivots around the corner to the left. He fires two shots immediately and by the time I step into the aisle the flashlight beam reveals a body on the ground.

I check behind us in the other direction. Even though I hear the gurgling growls of the dead in that direction, the aisle is still clear for the moment.

I take a couple steps backward and check over my shoulder to make sure I'm still close to the group.

Tim fires twice more behind me and I hear a groan before the dull thud of a body hitting the ground.

A pair of dark shapes finally emerge several aisles away from me. They lurch slowly, dragging their feet across the cement floor. I can't make out any details about them from here other than that, but I'm pretty sure they're dead.

We don't have much ammo to spare, so I steady the rifle and take my time to aim. Then I squeeze the trigger at the first dark figure. I adjust my aim a little higher and pull the trigger again. This time it tumbles to the floor, and I spot another one coming up the aisle behind it.

Bones whirls back toward me and starts shooting beside me at the other figures. Tim fires a few more shots, then I hear the quick rattle of Elise firing the submachine gun.

Tim stops advancing down the aisle and just crouches in the aisle in the center of the store. The dead know we are here now. We're not hunting them anymore. They're hunting us. We position ourselves in a tight circle, each covering the dead coming at us from a different direction of the store. Stitch darts into middle of us for protection and proceeds to bark repeatedly like he is giving us orders.

The dead continue to come at us from every direction. I focus on three more that are headed down the aisle I am covering. They stumble and clatter over everything in their path making it hard to get a lock on them for more than a second. I take a shot at the closest one, but he jerks awkwardly and the bullet sounds like it shatters a lighting fixture instead.

"Damn," I curse.

We don't have enough bullets to waste like that. I take a breath and wait until they close the distance, so I can make out their silhouettes better in the dark. Then I squeeze the trigger. I shift the rifle and fire again and again until nothing in the aisle moves any longer.

After the gunfire stops, we stay crouched in the middle of the store and listen to make sure we don't hear any more of them that might still be inside. The only sound I hear is a continuous dripping sound. I turn my head and glance down the aisle to see some of the bullet-riddled cans of paint on the shelves spill their contents on the floor.

"I think we got them all," Tim finally says. He stands up and lowers his rifle but keeps it ready in his hands. "Good work."

Stitch trots out from in between us and looks around at the store and wags his tail.

"Let's make sure the front doors are secure," he says.

We head down the aisle of the paint department, stepping over the paint splattered bodies on the ground.

"Jesus, Elise," Tim says. "You made an even bigger mess than you do at home."

"You're hilarious," Elise says.

Once we reach the service counter and realize the entrance of the store is still locked up tight, we take a minute to relax. Even though we can see the dead lined up and clawing at the front windows, for the moment we don't have to worry about any of them. Tim even sets his rifle down on the counter and takes a long look at the massive interior of the store.

"We did it," he smiles. "Look at this place."

I shrug off the backpack from my shoulders and drop it on the ground. It's not so easy for me to be excited. All I can think about is the fact that none of this stuff will do us much good when we're trapped inside and don't even have a vehicle to transport this stuff. Even though that's what I'm thinking I let Tim enjoy it for a moment.

"It's just a hardware store," Elise says. "We should have taken over a mall or something."

Tim looks at her, sees her smirk, and then lets out a scoffing laugh.

"I don't want to be a stick in the mud," Bones says. "But we're just about out of ammo, we have no vehicle, and this place is completely surrounded. So, what exactly is the plan to get us out of this?"

Tim lets her finish and then crosses his arms and leans back against a stack of parked shopping carts.

"Please tell me you have a plan," Bones says.

"I'm working on one," Tim says.

"Working on one?" Bones scoffs.

"Just keep cool, okay?" Tim says. "This isn't ideal, but we're safe for now. The situation is under control. We'll figure a way out of here."

He pauses for several seconds and stares at Bones until she finally responds.

"Okay," she agrees.

"For now, let's just have a look around," Tim says. "See what you can find that might be useful to us tonight. Sleeping bags, propane grills, stuff like that. I'm going to see if I can find a way up to the roof. See if I can get a better lay of the land out there."

"I'll come with you," I offer.

Tim looks at me and considers it for a second before he jerks his head to the side.

"Okay," he says. "Come on then."

We grab our rifles and then head back toward the loading area again. Tim walks a few paces ahead of me and I almost have to jog to keep up with him. He isn't the kind of guy that really likes to sit around for very long. I kind of noticed that the longer he sits somewhere, the more irritable he gets. He is a man that needs a mission.

In the back of the store, we locate a ladder on the wall the goes up to a hatch on the roof. I follow Tim up the ladder and then I realize Stitch is whimpering down below me. He must have trailed us back here and now is anxious that we are leaving him alone.

"Be right back, buddy," I tell him. "Go back up front."

He just cocks his head to the side and wags his tails. Idiot.

"Fine," I tell him. "Stay."

I continue climbing up the ladder behind Tim. He pushes open the roof hatch and the bright light of day blinds me momentarily. I close my eyes and feel blindly for the next couple of rungs of the ladder until I pull myself up onto the rooftop.

The whole roof of the building is covered in solar panels.

Tim and I look at each other for a moment. I can't tell if he is thinking what I'm thinking. There's a good chance we just need to flip a switch inside, and this place will have power again.

We walk between the solar panels until we reach the edge of the building. Only a couple of small snow-covered sedans sit in the front of the parking lot, but there are hundreds of the dead wandering just below us.

"That's not good," I say.

Tim doesn't respond. I turn to look at him and find he isn't looking at the dead. Instead, his eyes search the other buildings in the area.

"Over there," he points. "See that?"

"The shipping place?" I ask him.

"Yeah," he says. "See semi-truck in the lot. We can fit as much as we want in there. That's our ticket home."

CHAPTER THIRTEEN

While the solar panels on the roof might be good news, I'm still not so sure what to think about the idea of getting this truck across the street. I take another look at the shipping facility and the crowd of the undead that surrounds the building.

"There is no way," I mutter.

When I get no response, I turn around to find Tim is already descending back into the building. I head back inside with all the ways this will go wrong running through my mind. Maybe there is more to the plan.

"Tim," I say as I step off the bottom of the ladder.

He has located a fuse box and is checking the circuit breakers.

"What?" he says.

"I'm not sure how you want to go about getting over to that truck," I say. "I mean, the building is surrounded. But supposing we get over there, can you even drive that thing?"

"No," says Tim. "But Elise can."

"Elise," I say. "She is a truck driver?"

Tim stops inspecting the switches. He turns back to look and me and in the faint light from the open roof hatch, I notice his grin. Then he shakes his head slightly as he turns back to the electrical panel and flips a switch. The lights in the ceiling begin to hum and blink a few seconds later. Tim tilts his head up and basks beneath their glow for a moment.

"Elise might not look like your typical truck driver," Tim finally says. "But you've heard her talk. She started driving rigs when she was in the army. Got her CDL there. Been driving them ever since."

Tim pats me on the shoulder, clearly amused by the dumbfounded expression on my face. It's not really that I'm surprised a girl like Elise can drive a truck like that. Well, maybe a little bit. It's also that I suddenly realized it's been a couple of weeks and I still really am just getting to know all of them a little better.

If I'm being really honest, I'm back to avoiding getting to know anyone. After watching so many people I started to care about getting torn to shreds, it's just easier to pretend the people I don't really know don't matter to me. It's not really as bad as it sounds. I lived my life like that for years before all of this. You can think what you want. Maybe you think you're different, but you probably did it too.

"Holy shit!" Elise says. She runs into the stockroom with Bones right behind her. "The lights! How?"

"The roof is covered in solar panels," Tim informs her. "Saw a housing unit for the batteries and a chain of inverters mounted up there, so I figured the system was probably off-grid."

"I kind of want to stay here now," Elise says.

"With all those things outside we might not have a choice," I say.

Tim and Elise look at each other and fall silent again for a moment.

"He's right," Bones agrees. "This is good and all, but we need to start figuring out how we're going to get out of here."

"It's only a matter of time before those things get inside," I tell him. "They always do."

"Okay," he says. "I hear you."

He takes a few steps and looks around at all the shelves of merchandise and then his eyes finally settle on the overhead doors where the dead are still clawing against the metal surface to get inside. Tim exhales a long breath that plumes into the cold air in front of his face. Then he turns back around and looks at Bones.

"Look, everything we need is right here," Tim says. "Just down the block, there is an immediate care center. A grocery store. A gun shop. There is a parking lot full of semi-trucks across the street. All we have to do is get over there. Elise knows how to drive them. We can back it right up to these loading doors."

"It's probably not going to be that easy," I interrupt. "Hitting all those stores. Just the four of us."

"I never said this was going to be easy," Tim tells.

"How do you even know if the truck will still run?" Bones asks. "They might not even have enough fuel to get us back."

"I didn't say I have it all figured out," Tim says. He turns away from us and stares up at the ceiling and sighs.

I can tell Tim is getting defensive. As I am starting to learn, he is not really comfortable giving us orders. It is still kind of puzzling considering his past and experience. After we freed all those people at the prison, Tim made it clear he wanted nothing to do with being their leader. Maybe he just wants to be left alone like he says. I'm starting to think there must be more to it than that— some part of the story that I'm missing that would explain the reason he is this way.

"We're just trying to figure this out, too" I tell him before I turn and make eye contact with Bones. "No need to get all worked up. Let's just all keep cool."

Nobody says anything for a few seconds.

Stitch yawns and then sits down on the cold floor. He glances down and then decides to settle on his side, lifts his leg, and starts loudly licking himself.

"Really?" Elise says. "You're doing that right now."

Stitch senses us watching him and looks up at Elise. His tongue licks around the top of his mouth. Then he lowers his head, sniffs, and starts lapping noisily again. Stupid dog.

"Jesus," Elise sighs.

None of us are really laughing, but the distraction seems to take the edge off the tense moment.

Tim slowly turns back around. I notice his lips are still tensely pressed together, but then his hand comes up and covers his mouth. He exhales into his hand at first, as though to warm it from the cold, but then continues to cover his jaw and rubs at the stubble surrounding it while he stares pensively at a spot on the floor.

"For now, we're safe here," I continue. "We have power. We have everything we need to secure this place, right?"

Tim looks up at me and nods.

"I can keep those things out," he assures Bones.

"Bones," I say. "Maybe you and Elise can find some space heaters around here to help us stay warm tonight. We got power here, so we might as well use it."

The two of them nod in silent agreement.

"Okay," I say. "Let's get to work."

I stand there for a moment while Elise and Bones head for the sales floor and Tim watches them go. Then he slowly lowers his hand and uncrosses his arms.

"I'll go find some boards and nails," he says. "Bring them up front."

"Okay," I say. "I'll look for some tools. Meet you up there."

He walks by me and heads off on his mission. I watch him go and then allow myself to take a moment alone in the loading bay. I was much more comfortable when I felt like Tim had the situation under control. Now it feels like he might be in over his head.

I'm really not sure that I'm up for any of this. Even though I'm trying to keep us alive out here, I am starting to feel like the chance that we will never make it back alive is coming closer and closer to reality. The hardest part is, I'm starting feel a little too comfortable with that possibility to even trust myself to make the best decisions. I don't want anyone here dying because of me.

I make my way toward the tool department in the front of the store. The bodies of the dead are still lying all over the sales floor. I step over several of them as I cross the aisle that runs through the middle of the store. After staring at the shelf for a minute, I pick up a couple of hammers. Then I begin to open the box for a cordless drill, before I realize I probably don't want to sit around and wait for it to charge. I toss it back on the shelf and locate a drill with a cord instead. Then I search around the store for an extension cord. I find one in the electrical department, along with a coffee maker that I grab along the way. I nearly died carrying all that damn coffee here, so I might as well enjoy it.

By the time I get back up to the entrance, Tim is standing beside a pallet cart stacked high with plywood and boards and staring at the dead faces pressed up against the windows. They claw and bang on the glass. Even if the window has held them out so far, I can't help but feel anxious when I watch them trying to break through it.

"You think they can get through?" I ask him.

"It's holding up," he says. "Probably laminate glass. Pretty solid."

He turns and picks up a big piece of plywood off the cart and carries it up to the window.

"Still," Tim grunts. He pauses to set the wood down. "Better to be safe than sorry."

We work together to reinforce the windows and the doors. It takes a couple of hours to cover them all and reinforce the plywood with boards. When we finish, we grab a couple of sodas from a cooler near the checkout counter and stand there for a minute staring at the results. We can still hear the dead. They moan and bang on the glass. But at least we don't need to see them now. That alone is enough to make it feel safer inside here.

The two of us head back to find the ladies and Stitch sitting on some patio furniture situated around the glowing orange flame of a propane fire pit. I sit down on a wicker lounger to rest for a few minutes and enjoy the warmth of the fire. Stitch comes over and settles down next to me and curls into a ball and quickly falls asleep. I look over at the selection of grills and suddenly start to realize how hungry I am.

"I wish we had something to grill," I say. "I could go for a burger. Or a hot dog."

"A juicy bone-in ribeye steak," Elise suggests.

"Now we're talking," Tim says.

"What do we have to eat here anyway?" I ask.

"It's a hardware store," Elise says. "All we found was some candy bars, jerky and sunflower seeds from the registers."

"That's disappointing," I say. "Aside from the lack of food, this place is pretty nice."

"Aside from the reeking bodies all over the place," Elise says.

"Well yeah, there is still that," I say.

"There is a door on the other side of the store that leads to a fenced-in courtyard where they keep all the landscaping materials. Mulch and shit like that," Tim says. "We can move them out there in a minute."

He collapses into a patio chair and takes off the watch cap off his head and brushes his fingers through the sweaty brown hair that is plastered to his head.

"I just need a minute to rest," he says. "And start figuring out how we get out of here and get that truck."

"I was thinking," Elise says. "It seems like a shame to give up this place."

"We can't stay here," Tim says.

"I'm not saying we should move in here," Elise tells him.

"Then what are you saying?" Tim says.

"We can't possibly bring everything back that we're going to need on that truck," Elise says. "Not in one trip."

"We'll get as much as we can," Tim says. "We'll make do."

"What if we come back," she says. "You said it yourself, everything we could ever want is around here. So, some of us can come back. Gather everything we'll need from town. Store it in here until we need it."

"Or until someone else comes along and takes it," Bones says.

"Some of us could stay behind," Elise says. "To protect this place."

"That all sounds... ambitious," I say.

"That sounds like a lot of work," Tim says. "A lot of risk, too."

"Think about it," Elise says. "You know I'm right. We can only haul so much of this shit up the mountain and we don't have anywhere to store everything we're going to need. We need a better system. Instead of hunting around all over the place every time we run out of something, we will already have it all right here in one location. We can just back the truck up to the dock and load it up. Besides, we all know the house is too crowded. This is the best solution."

Tim leans forward in his chair and interlaces the fingers of his hands together and presses them against his lips and stares at the fire pit while he considers the idea for a moment.

"So?" Elise says. "What do you think?"

Tim lowers his hands and looks at Elise again.

"I think we're getting way ahead of ourselves," Tim says. "We'll get what we can carry and get the truck back to cabin. We can talk about it with everyone else then and decide what to do. It's a good idea, but we would need to get them on board to pull it off."

Tim gets up from his chair and walks away from the fire pit. I can't help thinking that if we had allowed those other people from the prison to come with us, we might have all the help we needed here. Maybe Tim can see that now too, or maybe he can't. Maybe he still wouldn't want to deal with them either way.

"Somebody going to come give me a hand with all these bodies?" Tim calls back.

As much as none of us want to, we all get ourselves out of our seats because there isn't anyone else here but us to do it.

CHAPTER FOURTEEN

When I wake up and look around, I discover that Tim is gone. I rub my eyes and sit there for a moment. I think it's morning. It feels like morning at least, although it is impossible to tell if the sun is up or down after we covered all the windows.

After several minutes of sitting in silence with no sign of Tim, I decide to get up and search for him. Even though we secured this place pretty well, I've learned that with the world the way it is now anything can happen.

A chill runs down my spine as I search the darkened aisles. The floor is still covered in debris and gore from our encounter with the dead inside the building yesterday. It gives me a bad feeling, but I tell myself it is just the cold. Even though it was pretty warm by the space heaters, the store still feels chilly when I wander a short distance away from them.

Tim doesn't seem to be anywhere on the sales floor, so I head for the back room. I push through the door to the warehouse and poke my head inside.

"Tim!" I whisper so loudly that it probably is not really a whisper.

There is no answer. The dead have stopped assaulting the loading bay doors and now the receiving area is completely silent. I make my way through the pallets and boxes by the light from the open hatch to the roof. I can see flakes of snow drifting down through the hatch. He must have gone back up to look around outside.

I climb up the ladder and onto the roof of the building with the fresh falling snow swirling in the air around me. A couple more inches of precipitation have accumulated on the roof already.

Tim sits on the ledge of the roof on the front side of the store. He stares at a black radio with a long whip antenna in his hand. I didn't even know he had a radio. He looks up when he hears me crunching through the snow.

"Is that a radio?" I ask him.

"Phone," Tim says.

"It still works?" I say.

"As long as the satellites are still up there," he says and jerks his thumb toward the sky.

"You find that here?" I say.

"No," he says. "I brought it along. My wife has the other, but she gave hers to Chuck before he left."

I'm kind of shocked they didn't feel they should tell me about this. It doesn't seem like he was trying to hide it or anything, but still. It seems like something kind of worth mentioning, I guess. Maybe he did mention it, and I just wasn't paying close enough attention. My mind has been pretty preoccupied lately, so it is possible.

"Oh, I didn't even know you had that," I say and then nod so he doesn't think I'm taking being kept out of the loop personally. "How are they doing?"

"I don't know he says," Tim says. "They're not responding."

Tim stops staring at the phone and lifts his head and stares at the mountains in the distance. I can tell he has a bad feeling and I start to get one as well.

"I told him I'd turn the phone on at dawn this morning to check in," Tim says.

Fletcher is a reliable person most of the time, but I've also been around him long enough to know that every once in a while, he will get himself in trouble by going off and doing his own thing. He still somehow always manages to come out of it without a scratch.

"It's Chuck," I tell him. "I'm sure he'll be fine."

"I hope you're right," he says.

Tim doesn't look reassured, but he nods his head silently anyway. He tilts his head back and stares at the clouds dropping snow down on us from the sky.

"All this snow is not going to make it any easier for us to get home," I say.

"We'll figure it out," Tim says. He turns his gaze to the truck across the road. "First things first."

"The truck," I say. "Have you figured out a way to get over there?"

I look over the edge at the dead out in the front of the store. About twenty or so of them are still pressed up against the front windows of the store. More of them shuffle around in the powder covering the parking lot.

"Not one that isn't dangerous," he says. "There are still a lot of them out front. The ones that were at the back door are mostly gone. Made their way up front with the rest of them, I guess. Hard to figure out any sort of reasoning behind their movements."

"That's because there isn't any," I say. "They'll probably stick around until something else gets their attention."

Tim stares down at the parking lot again.

"Makes it kind of hard to figure out how long it'll take to wait them out," he says.

I turn and walk across the roof to look at the lot behind the building. There are still maybe ten more corpses milling around the loading bay doors. I am pretty certain we can handle that many, but it would probably require us to make some noise. Then we'd have even more of them to deal with, and we don't have the ammunition for that kind of fight. I consider our options while I head back across the roof.

"A while back we were surrounded like this," I tell Tim. "It was a pharmacy. This guy took one of those remote-controlled cars and put a boombox on it. Used it to lure them away from the building."

"That worked?" Tim says.

"Got us out alive," I say. "Well, most of us at least."

"Most of you?" Tim says.

"Yeah," I admit.

"We don't have any RC cars," Tim says.

Tim shifts his eyes to the left and then to the right. Seems like it's more to avoid making eye contact with me than actually searching for something. I know he doesn't like my idea and is probably just trying to keep that opinion to himself, but I'm just trying to help him figure this mess out.

"So what are you thinking?" I ask him. "You want to try and wait them out?"

"We don't have time for that," Tim says.

He sits on the ledge and stares at the snow collecting on the roof all around us.

"Maybe we can use the landscaping center on the side of the store," Tim says. "The fence has a gate at the front of the store. We can open it up. Lure them inside somehow."

"Like a corral," I say.

"Yeah," Tim says. "It's big enough to hold most of the ones out front. Might not get them all in there but we can thin them out enough to clear ourselves a path."

"It's a pretty good idea," I tell him. "That could work."

"We need to move now," Tim says. "If this snow doesn't stop soon, we'll be trapped in here anyway."

Tim and I climb back down the ladder. I wait while he switches on the lights again. The big halogen bulbs near the ceiling come alive again and begin to hum. When we walk back out to the sales floor, I catch the scent of brewed coffee in the air. Elise and Bones are awake and eating breakfast. Stitch is still in a deep sleep on a patio cushion. He makes little yipping noises and runs in his sleep.

"Hurry up and finish eating," Tim says and accepts a cup of black coffee from Elise and thanks her.

Stitch jerks awake at the sound of Tim's voice and looks around the store. Then he yawns and lays his head down again and watches us from his warm cushion.

"What's going on?" Elise asks Tim.

"We figured out how we're getting out of here," Tim says before he gulps down half the cup of hot coffee. He swallows it down with a pained expression on his face.

"What is it?" Bones asks.

It seems like Tim needs a moment after burning his mouth, so I decide to fill them in on our plan.

"We're going to use the fenced lot on the side of the building," I tell them. "We think we can lure most of them inside. Lock them in there."

"Lure them in?" Bones says. "With what?"

"Someone will have to be the bait," Tim says.

All of us fall silent for a few seconds. No one seems to want to be the next one to speak. I think about it for a second, but there really is only one logical choice. Elise needs to drive the truck. Bones is the only one with any medical knowledge. Tim has a kid at home that needs a father.

"I'll do it," I finally say.

"You sure?" Tim says.

"Sure," I say. "No problem."

I try to play it off like it's nothing. I have done a lot of things that were probably way more dangerous since this all started. The only difference this time is that I'm volunteering to take the risks because I know I'm the one with nothing to lose. I am the most expendable of us.

"Okay then," Tim says. "We are going to have keep this quiet. No guns. Look for pipes, crowbars... anything that you can use to bash in their skulls."

"When are we doing this?" Bones asks.

"Right now," says Tim. "Snow started again. There's no way to know how much more is coming. So, we don't have time to waste. Let's go."

I head back toward the lumber department, checking down the aisles for anything that could be used to bludgeon the dead. I notice a few larger axes and walk over to pick one up. It's pretty heavy and feels like it would be a bit cumbersome to swing.

I catch a glimpse of something in my periphery and twist my head around to see Stitch sitting on the floor at the end of the aisle. He hangs back and eyes me holding the ax warily. When I put the ax back down, I spot some smaller hatchets on a shelf beside them. I retrieve one and test the weight and balance of it by swinging it a couple times. Much better. I grab one more, just in case, before I walk back down the aisle where Stitch is still waiting for me.

I get over to the garden center door and stare out at the dead bodies on the ground while I wait for the others. The corpses we put down yesterday and dragged out there are now all buried beneath a layer of fresh white snow. I know they used to be people, but after surviving this long, I feel like I've forgotten that fact. Maybe I just don't care anymore. It could be that I've become less human, too.

"Ready?" Tim says.

Tim has a coil of rope hung from one shoulder. He carries a duffel bag full of tools, a pair of bolt cutters, and a sledgehammer. Not sure he is going to need all that, but I guess he just wants to be prepared.

"I'm going up to the roof," he tells me. "Once you get them inside, I'll rope down and lock the gate back up. Good?"

"Got it," I say.

"You'll need these," Tim says and hands me the bolt cutters. "For the lock on the gate."

"Right," I say and tuck the handle of one of the hatchets under my arm to free my hand and take them from him.

"Where do you want us?" Elise says.

"You come with me," Tim says. "As soon as we lock those gates we'll run for the truck."

"And me?" Bones says.

Tim thinks about it for a second as he stares through the glass door and then he looks at me. I can tell he is not too sure I will make it back inside.

"You stay on this door," Tim tells Bones. "Wait for Blake to get back. Whatever happens, you make sure they don't get inside. Start boarding up the doorway right away after that."

"Copy that," Bones tells him.

"There's one other thing though," Tim says. "Once we get the truck, we might need to be ready to drive it back home right away."

"What about the grocery store," Elise says. "The other supplies."

"We'll just have come back for them," Tim says. "There are more than enough things we need in this place to fill up the trailer."

There is a long silence for a moment. We all look at Tim for a long moment and wait for him to go on.

"You said—" Elise begins.

"I know what I said," Tim cuts her off. "But the weather isn't getting any better out there. If we don't leave now—"

"It will pass," Elise says. "It's only October. You know in another day or two this snow will melt. It will be much easier to drive home then."

"We don't know that," Tim says. "Besides, I think we have taken enough chances out here already."

"Tim," Elise says. "I know you want to get back home. I do too. If we leave now though we are taking an even bigger risk by going on the road right now."

"Listen, Elise," Tim says. "I got a bad feeling something might have happened to Chuck."

"What do you mean?" she says.

Tim reaches into his jacket and pulls out the satellite phone.

"I haven't been able to get hold of them since we left," Tim says. "But it's not just that. I've had a bad feeling since we left. I should have never let him go off like that without me. If something happen—"

"Hey," Elise says. She takes a step towards her brother-in-law and lowers her voice to a whisper. "Look. I hear what you're saying. I do. But we're here. There isn't anything we can do about any of that right now. We need to wait to head back until after this storm clears. That's our only option. The roads are already a mess."

Tim lowers his eyes for a moment as he listens. I can tell he doesn't like what he is hearing, but he nods his head slightly as she goes on to acknowledge her point. He may not like it, but he is the reason we're all out here to begin with. This whole thing was his idea. He talked me into it coming here instead of continuing to search for Stevie with Fletcher and Scout. Now is not the time to start having second thoughts. It's too late for that.

"Alright," Tim relents. "You're the one driving the truck. You make the call when you think we it will be safe to drive home."

Elise smiles and reaches out to squeeze his hand gently and then pats him on the arm.

"Until then?" I ask.

"I guess we'll stick with the plan," Tim says. "Let's get to it then." He picks up the bag of tools and starts to walk toward the back of the store with Elise a few steps behind him. Stitch watches them go then looks back at us with his head cocked to the side.

I look at Bones and she smiles. Probably just to make me feel better about going out there and being the bait alone. It doesn't though.

CHAPTER FIFTEEN

"You sure you're okay doing this?" Bones asks me. "I can—"

"I'll be fine," I assure her. "If something goes wrong, don't hesitate to close the door on me."

I prop the bolt cutters against the glass door while I zip my coat up. When I go to retrieve them, I notice Stitch is right beside me, ready to run out the door. He stares up at me and waits for me to go.

"You stay here, little guy," I tell him and reach down to scratch him on top of his head.

Sure, I don't want him to get hurt. I also don't trust him not to do something totally stupid and get himself killed.

"Stay," I repeat.

Finally, I push the door open and run out into the swirling snow and nearly trip over the stupid dog when he bolts through the door right beside me.

"Stitch!" I yell. "Get back inside!"

The dog just sniffs the snow and then stares at me. Bones calls him from the door, and he looks at her then turns his head the other way. It is almost as though he is trying to find what we're yelling about. This kind of stuff is the exact reason I told the mutt to stay inside.

"Damn dog," I curse.

If he wants to die out here, that's his problem. I can't stand out here and yell at that idiot and bring every one of those things to the gate before I get it open. When I look toward the entrance, I notice a few of them are already approaching, probably drawn by the sound of me calling the stupid dog.

To hell with it.

I continue toward the gate, stepping over the dead bodies shrouded in a layer of snow. By the time I get to the gate, a corpse is already on the other side. The dead man puts his arms through the bars of the fence and reaches for me. He tries to stick his head through as well, but the gap is just narrow enough to stop him.

For a moment, I stand there and stare the hideous pale face of the dead man while he opens his mouth and chomps on the air. I can't figure out how I'm going to use the bolt cutters on the lock without getting too close.

More of them are getting near. I drop the bolt cutters for a moment and take one of the hatchets in my good hand and crack the dead man in the skull with the blade as hard as I can. The guy slumps to the ground and I quickly scoop up the bolt cutters again.

Several more corpses are closing in on the gate. I only have a few seconds before they reach the fence. I get the bolt cutters on the lock and start to squeeze. Nothing happens. I'm not the strongest guy in the world. Adrenaline kicks in when I look up as the frost-covered corpse of a woman slams into the fence. The metal gives way and the lock pops free and falls to the ground with a clang.

An instant later, the gate swings open and nearly hits me as I retreat backwards. The dead stumble inside, moaning and stretching their arms out in front of them to try and grab onto me. Even though I am off balance, I swing the bloody hatchet at a dead woman with long hair and half the skin eaten off her face. It does enough damage to drop her to the ground, but the blade lodges in her cranium and I lose my grip on the handle as she tumbles to the ground.

Stitch barks somewhere behind me.

"Get the hell out of there!" I hear Tim yell from up above me.

As I turn to run for the doors, another corpse grabs my left arm— the arm that is still holding the other hatchet. I try to jerk it free, but the thing has both hands clamped on me. I switch the hatchet to my right hand and bring it up to hack at the thing. Before I do, I feel more fingers grabbing at my right leg.

I start to panic and yell as I swing the hatchet down wildly at the corpse hanging on my arm. The dead woman falls to the ground, but another corpse immediately grabs my sleeve. I try to tug my limbs free from dead hands that seem to have a hold of me everywhere now.

Stitch darts into the fray. He barks and snaps his jaws on the jacket of a dead soldier that has his pale icy hands wrapped around my ankle. Another one of them grabs onto the hatchet, so I don't really have much choice but to let it take it. There is no time to fight them over it. As soon as I get one of my hands free again, I unzip my coat and slip out of it to free myself from the clutches of the dead.

The moment I break away, I head for the door where Bones is waiting for me. Her face is pale, and her mouth is open as she watches in horror. I don't even need to look back. From seeing the look on her face, I know the dead are right behind me.

My boots slide on the slick layer trampled snow that covers the pavement, but I manage to step over the frozen bodies on the ground without losing my footing. When I reach the door, I hear Stitch bark again. I turn around to search for him and when I realize he isn't right behind me I glance around the garden center before I run inside. I watch the dead stumbling over the bodies on the ground. They crawl forward, tripping up the others right behind them. My eyes quickly scan the bags of mulch and topsoil, but I don't see the little mutt.

"Stitch!" I call out.

No sign of the stupid dog anywhere.

The dead continue to pour through the gate. They trample over dead plants and bodies to get to me. In my head, I quickly estimate the few seconds it will take them to get here. I have to move if I don't want to die.

Finally, Stitch hops onto a stack of bags on the far end of the lot. He watches the dead coming inside with his mouth open and his tongue sticking out. His rapid panting makes tiny white puffs in the cold air. Stitch turns his head and looks at the dead and then makes eye contact with me for a moment. I know there is no way he can get back to the door in time.

"Blake!" Bones pleads. "Get in! Come on!"

Stitch barks at me then, too. It's like he is telling me to get my ass inside.

The dead are just a few feet away from me now. I don't want to leave him out there, but I know I don't really have a choice. So, I spin around and run through the door.

By the time we push it shut, the dead are already pressed up against the other side of the glass. Bones and I throw ourselves against the other side to stop them from shoving it back open. I try not to look at the terrifying faces of death biting on the other side of the glass while I flip the deadbolt.

Once the door is locked, we step back and stare at it for a moment. There is no telling how long it might hold. I look for any sign of Stitch outside, but there are too many bodies blocking the way now. My stomach twists into a knot and a coppery taste fills my mouth. I know he is just a dog, but he has risked his hide for me so many times. I'm feeling sick about leaving him out there.

"Nothing you could have done," Bones tells me.

It might be true, but it doesn't help right now. I take another look at the things on the other side of the glass. Maybe they have no idea what they're doing anymore, but I can't help but hate them. In this moment, I just want to destroy them all. It doesn't matter if they used to be people. Now, they're just monsters. I might not have much to live for anymore, but that doesn't mean I am willing to give up and let them win. That's why I can't act like losing Stitch out there bothers me, even though it really does bother me.

"Let's just get the door secured," I say to Bones. "We don't have time to worry about that idiot."

Bones looks at me and opens her mouth to speak but then bites her lip as I walk by her and head for panels of plywood stacked against the wall. When I grab the first board, I realize she is still staring at the dead through the glass. She isn't crying, but the sunlight reflects off her watery eyes. She blinks a few times before she turns and hurries down the aisle to help me lift the plywood.

We carry it over and lean it against the door. The dead continue to assault the glass even as we block it off so they can no longer see us. The two of us go back down the aisle for another board even though I'm sucking wind. After we lean six more panels against the door, we can only barely hear the thudding fists and muffled moans of the dead outside. We stand back and look at the barricade and catch our breath.

"We can slide some appliances over to reinforce it," I say. "It should be enough to keep them out."

"Do you think they made it?" Bones asks me.

Even though I know what she means, I think about it for a moment.

"We didn't hear any shooting," I say. "That's probably a good sign."

"Right," Bones says.

"Let's finish securing this door and then we'll go up on the roof and check it out," I say.

It takes us another ten minutes to push some heavy display appliances onto a pushcart and wheel it back to the garden center door. We are both dripping sweat by the time we tip the pair of refrigerators upright again and slide them back against the sheets of plywood.

"That should hold," I say, even though I'm not really sure it would last forever. "At least for now."

"Yeah," Bones agrees and wipes the sweat off her brow with the sleeve of her sweatshirt.

"Let's go up on the roof," I say.

We walk towards the receiving bay and head for the maintenance ladder. After we climb up, we make our way across the roof to the front corner of the building. Secured to one of the solar panel mounts is a rope that is hanging over the edge of the roof.

I look down and see the garden center down below. The gate is closed and secured with a chain and padlock again. A couple of bodies lie on the ground below. Their skulls are bashed open, and the contents are splattered on the snow. There are still a small number of corpses wandering in the front lot, but most of the ones that were out there took the bait and came through the gate. From the look of it, there must be over a hundred corpses locked inside the courtyard.

I look around, but there is no sign of Stitch down there. Maybe that's a good thing. I don't see fresh blood anywhere. At least it doesn't look like the things ate him. The bars of the fence are wide enough that he may have been able to slip through them and escape. Either that, or he found some place to hide down there. Maybe I am trying to convince myself the dog is okay even though I don't really believe it. I've learned not to hope for things like that after everything I've been through.

"Look!" Bones says and pats her hand on my shoulder several times to get my attention. She is pointing to the shipping center across the road.

Then I see the two figures running across the snow toward one of the semi-trucks, and the scruffy little dog running right behind them. The dog stops for a moment and turns to look back as though he can sense our eyes on him. Then he races to catch up with Tim and Elise again.

"They made it," Bones says. "All of them."

It takes a few seconds for me to believe what I'm seeing. When it finally sinks in, I smile for the first time in quite a while.

From across the street, we barely hear the engine of the truck starting up over the blustering winds. As much as the weather might make it difficult to get home, it will likely help to drown out any noise we make that could attract more of the dead.

A cloud of exhaust spits from the pipe alongside the front of the cab and the truck rumbles forward through the snow.

"They got it started," Bones says. "Holy shit."

Several corpses that are close enough to hear the truck start to wander toward the entrance. I can just barely see Elise behind the steering wheel and Tim beside her. She doesn't even try to avoid hitting the dead as the truck accelerates. The wheels slide over the snow as she takes the turn out of the parking lot. Then she eases off the gas before the truck jackknives and coasts ahead toward the entrance to the hardware store lot.

I look down at the corpses in the garden center below when I hear the padlocked chains on the gate begin to rattle. They have all wandered away from the door to the building and are pressed against the front of the fence and reaching through the bars as the truck cuts across the parking lot.

"Let's get back downstairs," I tell Bones as the truck heads around the side of the building.

I follow her across the roof again and we climb back down the ladder. As I descend, rung by rung, trying to make sure my icy hands don't lose their grip on the slick metal, I hear the truck beep as it begins to back up to the loading bay door.

By the time we make it to the bottom of the ladder, the rumbling truck engine has stopped outside. I hear a door slam, then another.

"Go!" I hear Tim say. "Get inside!"

"Open the door!" Elise yells.

I can hear Tim grunt and then the dull impact of something getting hit with a blunt object. Elise starts to bang on the door just as we get there to pull it open.

The truck is backed up to the loading bay door just to the right of the one that I opened. It is covered in months of dirt and dust, but I can still make out the faded brown and yellow eagle logo on the side of the trailer. The tires are splattered with fresh gore and clumps of icy snow.

Elise picks up Stitch and he squirms awkwardly in her arms as she sets him on the ledge. Then she reaches up and we each grab one of her arms and pull her up into the loading bay.

Tim is still fighting off a couple of frosty corpses in the snow. He cracks one guy with a long beard across the face. Icy congealed blood sprays up into the air when the lead pipe lands and sends the dead guy sprawling on the ground. The other man grabs Tim by the arm and tries to bite him through his winter jacket.

"Look out, Tim!" Bones yells even though Tim is probably all too aware of the situation he is in.

Tim slugs the other corpse in the face with his fist. Its head snaps to the side but it still grips his arm. He punches it again and again until it finally falls away. Even though it is still getting back up, Tim leaves it and runs for the loading dock. There are just a few more of the dead remaining in the back alley, but they are all converging on the doors now. I step to the side as Tim lunges onto the ledge and swings his legs up then rolls inside. As soon as he is clear, I pull the handle on the overhead door, and it rolls down and slams loudly against the concrete.

The dead bang the metal door with their hands a moment later. The sound echoes loudly in the quiet stockroom.

I sit on a box to catch my breath and give Stitch a pat on the head when he starts to lick my hand.

"We did it," Elise pants.

I look up to see her sitting on the floor with her back against a pile of boxes. She twists the cap off a water bottle and takes a sip. Beside her, Tim lies on the floor. He breathes hard as he stares up at the lights on the ceiling. He lifts his head slightly, looks over at Elise, and opens his mouth to speak, but still seems to need a minute to catch his breath. Elise holds out the water for him and he takes it but just holds the bottle in his hand for a minute.

"We fucking did it," Elise says again with a big smile on her face this time.

Tim smiles back but just holds up a hand with his palm up. Elise looks at it and then slaps him five.

"Good work," Tim finally manages to say. He groans and pushes himself up to a sitting position again and looks at the closed loading bay door. We sit there silently for several more minutes until the adrenaline subsides and then we get back to work.

CHAPTER SIXTEEN

T im leans over and puts his ear against the metal door and listens for several seconds. We each have two rounds in our handguns, and less than half a magazine for one assault rifle, which Tim has slung over his shoulder. With any luck, we won't need to shoot at all.

"You ready?" Tim looks back at the three of us and waits until we acknowledge him with a nod.

"Let's go," Elise says.

I adjust my grip on the steel pipe. It might not be enough to take care of one of those things permanently, but it can knock them down for a moment and keep them at a distance.

Tim grabs the strap on the bottom of the overhead door and heaves it up. The glare of the bright morning sun reflecting off the snow hits my eyes. I turn my head for a second because it actually hurts to look at the world outside.

Last night, the snowstorm finally relented. The snow on the ground is still nearly a foot deep, but it seems like the air outside is warmer today. If we're lucky the snow might even start to melt beneath the afternoon sun. We might even be able to return home tomorrow, assuming we live that long.

We hop down off the loading dock and into the snow. Stitch immediately starts to growl at the dead. The few corpses that had been banging on the door yesterday are scattered around the lot now. They all slowly turn to look at the loading dock doors again and stumble toward us through the drifts of snow.

Tim pulls down the door and jumps down to the pavement behind us. Several of the dead are already near the cab of the truck even though the snow is slowing them down.

"Under here," Elise says and crouches under the trailer.

We all follow her lead and avoid the dead by crossing beneath the truck to the other side and then we make a run for the street. Stitch hops along ahead of us, leaping like a goddamn gazelle through the snow. His tongue flops out of the side of his open mouth. He is still a dog, and he loves the snow.

Aside from the dead that we have trapped in the landscaping center, there are still only a few corpses in the vicinity. The gun shop is only across the street and halfway down the next block. We should be able to make it there without too much trouble. The only thing I am really worried about is whether we will be able to get inside.

We run up the incline toward the road and then scurry across the street. About fifteen or twenty corpses are around the intersection. Even though they see us coming, the snow slows them down so much that it is easy enough for us to run through them. I watch one woman with long brown dreadlocks and a long, tattered flower dress tumble over the curb and crash on her face in the snow.

At the corner, we turn left and head straight down the middle of the street. The gun shop comes into view up ahead. It is just a solid white building with GUNS painted in large black letters over the door. You can tell nobody ever had to have a catchy business name or attractive storefront to sell weapons in this country. There are no windows on the outside of the building at all. A pair of glass doors in the front show no signs of obvious damage.

Several blocks ahead, countless figures wander in the road. They're far enough away that they aren't likely to notice us as long as we don't do anything to draw their attention.

With his long strides, Tim is first to reach the front doors. He jerks on the handle and looks shocked when it actually opens. Then he nearly falls backwards when a corpse emerges through the doorway a moment later.

The dead man is almost as tall as Tim, but heavyset, and has a massive gunshot wound that has eviscerated his upper body. The thing latches on to him, but Tim manages to use the long handle of the sledgehammer like a bar to keep the guy off him.

"Get inside," he orders us when we move to help him. He pivots and tries to redirect the corpse away from us.

Instead of going inside, I raise the pipe over my shoulder and bring it down on top of his head with all the force I can manage. I hear a crunch as his skull gives in and then his arms go limp, and he collapses to the ground.

"Hurry," Elise holds open the door and waves her arm to urge us to run inside. A few corpses that had been standing around the area are now trudging toward us. I turn to run inside, and Tim pushes my back to move me in faster. Elise pulls the door shut behind us and flips the deadbolt just before the dead assault the entrance.

After being outside, with the bright sunlight glinting off the snow, it takes a moment for my eyes to adjust to the dark and gloomy interior of the gun shop. There was one of those things in here. There could be some more.

The only sound is that of Stitch panting loudly to catch his breath. The fact that Stitch seems more concerned about the corpses outside the door than anything in here puts my mind at ease.

Nothing moves among the display cases and the racks of tactical and hunting apparel on the sales floor. Rifles hang on racks above the dusty sales counter. Elaborate cobwebs stretch from the barrel of one rifle to the stock of another.

This place looks like it has been abandoned for ages even though it has only been six months. Empty racks on the wall and several smashed display cases indicate that looters had been here before, but there is still plenty left for us to take.

I take my eyes off the store and turn my head toward the others. Elise and Bones exchange smiles while Tim scans the guns with his mouth open. No one says anything at all for a few seconds. We just stand there and take it in until Tim finally tilts his head back. With his face toward the sky, he closes his eyes.

"Thank you," he whispers so softly that I can't hear him over the sound of the dead banging on the door but can only read his lips.

"Let's go shopping," Elise says.

"I'll check the back," I tell them.

First, I grab a coat off the rack to replace the one I lost while fighting off the corpses yesterday. Then, I walk to the sales counter but stop when I see what is on the floor behind it.

A pair of bodies are sprawled on the floor. The first one, dressed all in bloody denim and completely missing a head, slumps against the wall. A shotgun rests in his lap. The other body is just an eviscerated mess. Dried blood and rotten tissue in a pile on the floor.

As much as I want to turn around and try to forget that I ever saw this, the only way to see what is in the back of the store is by walking behind this counter to get to the stockroom door. I try not to look at the headless man as I step over his lifeless legs blocking my path. My boots squish through the congealed remains of the other body. Even if they have been here for months, it hasn't been long enough. Now that I've seen it, it will always be there. Time and nature can erase the most horrific things much better than the human mind can.

I grip the doorknob and my fingers feel the crusted dried blood on the handle. It makes me a bit squeamish just because I know exactly what I'm touching. After I crack the door open an inch to peek inside and see nothing but total blackness, I push the door wide open. I pull out a flashlight and the rubber button clicks beneath my finger when I press it. A beam of light shines on stacks of boxes and racks of guns. There looks to be enough guns and rounds of ammunition to take out half the town of Pueblo.

Unfortunately, there is no way we can carry it all right now. At least we can take enough with us to get us home. We can come back for the rest later. I still don't know if I really like our chances of surviving the winter, but we definitely have a better shot now.

We refill all our magazines and stuff as many boxes of ammo as we can carry into our backpacks. Will have to wait until we come back later to get more guns. We already have enough weapons, but ammunition is always a problem.

While looking through the boxes in the back room, I come across the back exit of the store. I pause by the metal door and try to listen for any sounds on the other side, but don't hear anything. At least the dead aren't hammering their fists and moaning to get inside like the ones are at the front door. Tim comes into the back room and shines his flashlight over the boxes until he notices me by the door.

"You good?" he says.

"We got out way out," I say and jerk my thumb to indicate the door. "Sounds clear out there for now."

"Good," Tim says. He grabs a box off the shelf and checks the label, then tucks it under his arm. "Man, this place is a gold mine. Shame we can't take more right now. If only—"

"We had more people here to help?" I interrupt.

The cone of his flashlight stops moving and shines on an empty spot on the concrete floor for several seconds. I can barely make out his facial features in the dim light, but I can feel him staring at me.

It might have been a couple days, but I haven't forgotten about the people at the prison. I can't help but wonder if they are even alive now. We also could have used their help here.

"You're still stuck on that, huh?" Tim finally says.

"A little bit," I tell him. "Those people could have really helped us. We could have really used them."

"So, you just wanted to use them?" Tim says. "Then we'd be no better than those Reapers."

"Not like that," I say. "You twisted my words. I meant we could help each other."

"I used to say the same thing to people when I was in Iraq," Tim says.

"This is different," I tell him.

"There isn't as much difference as you'd think," Tim says. "Look, Blake, as much as I'd enjoy standing around all day and arguing over this with you, we need to get the hell out of here while we still can. Pack up. Let's go."

He walks back out to the sales floor and leaves me in the dark and wondering if maybe I am looking at things the wrong way. We have survived so far by working together with everyone we could. I know it has helped keep me alive, but I can't say the same for most of the others.

Most of them are dead now.

I stare at the boxes of ammo sitting on the shelf beside me for a minute, but the only thing I see are all the faces of the people that have been lost since society collapsed. The worst part is, I know there will be more. I close my eyes for a second to try and push these thoughts away. When I open them again, I start grabbing boxes of ammunition.

I check the caliber of the bullets and try to remember which ones we need and which ones we don't. A few moments later, the faces are gone. Keeping my mind busy is the best way to avoid the dark thoughts lurking inside. After I shove as many boxes as my bag will hold, I zip it closed and haul it onto my back just as the others return from the front of the store.

The bag is really heavy. I was so preoccupied grabbing everything I could that I didn't really stop to think how hard it would be to carry.

"You got that?" he asks me when he sees me struggling. "Looks like you're carrying more than you can handle."

"It's not very far," I tell him. "I think I can make it."

"You might slow us down too much," he says.

"Don't worry about me," I say. "I can handle it."

I say this even though I'm not really sure that I can handle it.

Tim looks back over his shoulder toward Elise and Bones.

"Whatever happens, don't stop. Keep moving." Tim tells them.

Then he walks over, places his hand on the doorknob, and cracks the door open slightly to peek outside.

"It's clear," he whispers. "Let's go."

CHAPTER SEVENTEEN

Icy drops of melting snow dribble down on us from the roof as we slip out of the service entrance of the gun store. The back alley is still clear, but those things up front are still moaning loudly and pounding their fists against the windows. It helps to cover the noise of our clattering gear and boots crunching through the snow. We might even get out of here without drawing too much attention, which would be ideal since I am really struggling beneath the weight of the ammo I am carrying.

I pause next to a rusted van parked on the side of the building. Tim looks back at me and he knows he was right. Trying to carry this much was stupid. He doesn't say anything and pretends not to notice me hunched over and sweating as I try to keep up.

I grit my teeth until my jaw hurts. Pain is my friend in moments like this. Anger, too. I've learned that triggering pain or anger puts the body into survival mode. Then the adrenaline takes over.

Luckily, there seems to be no shortage of pain or reasons to be angry anymore. I just need to pick my poison. There is plenty of fuel to keep those fires going. The causes of our suffering are also what keep us alive. It makes me wonder how this all ends.

My boots are soaked and start to feel heavier with each step. I can hear the dead around me. but I just keep my eyes focused on the road ahead and try not to fall too far behind the group.

Even though I am losing ground, I push forward through the slushy snow by thinking of all the things that I try to forget except in these moments. Sometimes I envision the lifeless thing that was once my daughter outside her school. Other times, I see Danielle shambling through the smokey tunnels beneath Cheyenne Mountain. There is no shortage of horrifying memories to pick from in my mind.

The only problem is that when I open my mind to let them in at times like this, I can't turn them off. They can be so overwhelming. I feel like I am drowning in them. And when that happens it becomes impossible to focus on what is going on around me until something pulls me back into the moment like the cold hands of the dead.

"Blake!" Tim skids to a stop when he looks back again and realizes how far I have fallen behind them. Stitch is standing there in the road, barking his head off at me, too.

"I'm good," I say. But as soon as the words leave my mouth, the weight on my back suddenly becomes much heavier. I don't even need to look. I already know what is happening.

Bones and Elise notice the trouble I am in and start to run back but Tim holds out his arm to stop them.

"Keep going," he tells them.

"Tim," Elise says.

"Don't argue with me," Tim nudges her shoulder to urge her to move.

"Go!" I yell. I don't think I want to die, but I know I don't want them to die trying to save me either.

Tim turns back and I see a look of panic on his face as he runs back for me.

That is the last thing I see before the weight becomes too much. I tumble backwards but twist my body as I struggle desperately to free myself. I notice another corpse just as it lunges for me and crashes into the back of my legs. Then the dead tackle me to the ground awkwardly and I shut my eyes as I fall face first in the snow. Within seconds, there are several of them on me. I thrash around in the snow to keep them from grabbing on to me. I even hurl obscenities as a last futile attempt to break free, because deep down I already know I can't fight them all off this time. Everything goes dark when another one piles on me, and my face is buried beneath the putrid stench of his rotting flesh.

This is my own damn fault. I knew I was trying to carry too much weight. It wasn't stupid. I was just too stubborn to admit I was wrong. Still trying to show the macho tough guy that I'm just as much of a man. So goddamn stupid. I never learn.

Just as I give up and stop trying to fight them off, I feel a change in crushing weight of the bodies on top of me. Someone is pulling them off me. Tim grunts as he hauls another one off me and a moment later, I hear the dull thud of a body falling in the snow.

I realize I can move my arms and legs once again, so I start pushing the snarling dead man off my face. I don't know why Tim decided to risk his ass to come back and help me. I wouldn't blame him if he left me behind. He even told me he was going to. Since he is risking his ass, I feel like I should make sure it isn't for nothing. The last thing I want is one more person getting killed because of me.

Once I roll the corpse off me, I feel the layer of gore coating my face. The murky sludge drips off my chin onto the white snow. Fingers claw at my leg, and I look down to find another corpse trying to bite my calf. I kick at the thing several times until it releases me and then Tim grabs my arm and helps pull me up. I reach for the heavy bag of ammo on the ground but one of the corpses is tangled in the straps.

"Forget it," Tim says. "Just leave the damn thing."

"Damn it," I say and release the bag of ammo and turn to run away. There are dozens of corpses moaning and plodding through the snow all around us. I can feel them closing in and know that we had no other choice but to leave the backpack. Still, I glance back at it lying there in the middle of the road.

"We can go back and get it later," Tim pants. "Don't you even—"

"I'm not!" I tell him.

We slide down the grass embankment and cross the parking lot of the hardware store. By the time we circle around to the back of the building, the dead have fallen about fifty yards behind us. Elise and Bones wait inside the open door of the loading dock.

For a moment, the women stare with their mouths open at the sight of me covered in guts and blood running just behind Tim. I glance over my shoulder again, but there is nothing behind me. I wonder what they look so concerned about. Then I realize that it is just the sight of me. I probably look like a goddamn corpse. As we approach the loading dock, they see me running and realize I'm still very much alive. They give us a hand climbing up the platform. Then Elise pulls down the sliding bay doors that rattle and hit the ground with an echoing boom.

"Are you guys okay?" Elise asks.

"I think so," Tim says between gasps.

I can hardly speak so I just collapse onto the floor and stare up at the rafters while I catch my breath. I am still not really sure I am even okay. My body is numb from the cold, and I am covered in blood, so it's possible that some of it could be mine. I won't know for sure until I clean myself up. Bones approaches me with a look of concern on her face, but I wave her off.

"I just need a minute," I tell her.

"I'm going to start loading up the truck," Elise tells Tim.

"Right behind you," Tim tells her and holds up a finger.

With the sleeve of the new coat that I grabbed at the gun store, I wipe the guts and wretched filth off my face as much as I can. I take a moment to look at my arms and legs. I still can't believe that none of those things managed to sink their teeth into me.

"You good?" Tim says.

"I think so," I say, and then I look up to see Tim pulling up his sleeve and inspecting a wound on his forearm. The sight of the blood trickling down his arm hits me like a knife slicing open my belly. He twists the cap off a bottle of water and dumps it over the wound to clean it up. A metallic taste climbs up the back of my throat and I swallow it down to speak.

"Is that—"

"Not sure. Looks like it's just a cut," he says and pulls his sleeve back down to cover it. "I'm not really sure how it happened."

"You shouldn't have come back for me," I tell him.

"You saying that because you feel guilty or because you made up your mind to get yourself killed out here?" Tim says.

Caught off guard by the statement, I just sit there quietly and the two of us stare at each other for a long moment. I can't deny that what I did was reckless and stupid. It was also not the first time I did something that could have cost someone their life. I live with this, which is why the value of my own life doesn't mean as much to me anymore.

"Why did you come back?" I ask him. "You're always talking about how you don't want to be responsible for anyone."

"I don't," he says.

"So..." I say.

"I wasn't about to let Elise or Bones go back for you," he says. "I didn't exactly have a choice."

We fall silent again. Tim drinks the last few gulps from the water bottle before he tosses it a few feet away. I get the feeling that what he is telling me isn't entirely true when Tim lowers his gaze to avoid looking me in the eyes. I can tell that isn't the only reason, but it's just the reason he is willing to give.

"There's something you're not telling me," I say.

Tim falls silent for a moment that stretches to a full minute. It seemed like there should be more to the story, but he doesn't seem to have any intention of going on. His eyes just stare at the empty water bottle resting sideways on the cold concrete floor.

"Did Chuck ever tell you what went down in Juarez?" he finally asks.

I shake my head.

"My unit had been down there for six months for Operation Dark Shadow to take down Castillo," Tim says. "We burned his processing facilities and busted his shipments, but we couldn't get close to Castillo himself. He was like a ghost."

"Finally," Tim says, "we received intel from a reliable informant that Castillo was hiding out in this crappy hotel outside of Juarez. The only problem was the corrupt Mexican authorities wouldn't authorize a warrant. Everyone knew this was going to be our only shot to take him down, so command authorized a black operation."

Tim lifts his eyes to meet mine again. Then he turns his head and stares at the girls working together to load supplies into the truck. He seems to regret starting this conversation.

"It was completely off the books," Tim says. "We knew if shit went sideways that we would have no support. Nothing. But after six months down there we had seen enough bodies. We knew what Castillo was capable of and someone had to stop him."

"So," he says. "We went to the hotel. Had a visual I.D. on Castillo and his top sicario. It was a go. The only problem was somebody tipped them off. When we raided the building, the cartel was waiting for us. Worst firefight I ever been in. We took heavy casualties, but we got to Castillo. Took him alive. Then the cartel reinforcements showed up. Corrupt police."

Tim pauses his story for a moment and takes a deep breath.

"Then we're the ones trapped in the hotel. All shot up. Running out of ammo." Tim says. "Finally, shit got so bad the President called in the

Mexican Marines to restore order. Next thing I know I'm waking up in a Mexican hospital with three bullets in me and the rest of my team is dead."

After hearing all that, I feel like I understand him a bit more.

"I'm sorry, Tim," I say.

He holds up his hand in a vague gesture of acknowledgement.

"I'm done losing people, Blake," he says. "I already lost too many."

"I get it," I say. "I lost a lot of people too."

Tim looks at me for a long moment and then he nods his head in understanding. He turns and looks at Elise and Bones carrying a large panel of plywood into the trailer.

"We should go give them a hand," he says and pushes himself up from the floor and kicks the toe of his boot against the ground to clear off the clumps of muddy snow.

CHAPTER EIGHTEEN

With the weapons, ammo, and all the hardware supplies loaded, there isn't much room at all left in the truck. The dead that followed us back from the gun store are still gathered outside. They bang on the truck and moan loudly after hearing us move around.

"We can fit a little more," Tim says. "There is plenty more stuff sitting around in here that we can use anyway. Let's finish loading up as much as we can."

"There isn't much room for the food in there," Elise says.

"After that close call I'm not so sure we want to risk that," Tim says. "We should probably just get the medical supplies and get out of town."

"We're going to need more food, though," Elise says.

"I know we do," Tim agrees. He puts his hands on his hips and stares at the loaded trailer. "But we don't need food that bad. We can make do with what we have for now. We'll come back when we have more help."

"This is about Chuck and the others, isn't it?" Elise says. "You're still worried about them."

"It's about everything," Tim says. "But that's part of it for sure."

He glances at me quickly and smiles slightly as though to say he hasn't changed his mind because of me, but it still seems like that is exactly what happened from my perspective.

"Okay," Elise says. "That's your call I guess but we still can't drive in this snow."

"Yeah," Tim says. "I know. We'll get the medical supplies and wait here one more night. Head back in the morning."

"How we going to get out with all those things out there now?" I ask.

Tim picks up his rifle and ducks his head beneath the shoulder strap.

"We'll shoot our way out," Tim says. "We have the ammo now."

"That'll draw a lot of attention," Bones says.

"Duh. These things are all in the back now," Elise says. "We'll just go up to the roof and use the rope to go down in the front again."

The rest of us look at each other. The solution seems so obvious to us now even though it only occurred to Elise.

"Okay, hotshot," Tim says and then he gestures to the ladder on the wall. "Lead the way."

I grab my rifle and turn to climb up the ladder when I see Stitch staring up at me. There isn't really any way to bring him along with us, so I bend down and pet him on the head.

"Not this time, buddy," I say. I fish a piece of jerky out of my pocket and offer it to him. He looks up at me for a couple seconds before he gently takes the piece from my finger. Then he finds a spot to curl up and lays his treat down. I start to climb to the roof and listen as he whimpers and then starts to yap desperately when I go outside.

We all walk across the roof and check the front of the building. There are just a handful of corpses wandering in the parking lot out front and we have a pretty clear path to the minute clinic up the road.

"Looks like a piece of cake," says Tim.

"Don't say that," I say to Tim.

"I thought you weren't superstitious," he says.

I just shake my head. Tim laughs and pats me on the shoulder.

"Okay listen," he says. "Smash and grab. We get in. We get out. Those things will smash right through that glass, so we have to be quick. Bones, you just grab whatever you need, and we'll buy you as much time as we can."

He hands the rope to Elise and then she wraps it around her waist and climbs on the ledge. She turns around then repels down.

"You got this," he says. "No sweat. Just stay frosty this time."

He hands me the rope and then I get up on the ledge and lean back and start to ease myself down. I'm not exactly experienced at this sort of thing, so I nearly fall off twice and end up with a rope burn on my hands before I get to the bottom.

"Damn it," I curse under my breath.

That's when I realize if those things are outside when we get back, I'm going to have to go up the same way I came down while carrying whatever supplies we return with.

Elise takes a shot at an approaching dead cheerleader with a chunk of her face missing. She is still even holding on to a bloody pompom and waves it as us as she moans. The first shot misses, but Elise tags her with the next shot on she drops face down in the melting snow.

I pull out my pistol and keep it ready, but the parking lot is still empty. The dead inside the garden center just a few feet away are all riled up though now. They reach through the bars and moan and snap their teeth at us. Their presence makes me feel like we're in a lot of danger at the moment even though there aren't really any imminent threats.

Bones lands on the ground in between the two of us and then looks down at her hands and grits her teeth. She must not have done a lot of repelling in autopsy technician school.

Tim hits the ground a few seconds later, and then we all start running through the parking lot. It doesn't take long after the gunshots for more corpses to appear from all directions, but we get through the parking lot without having to fire another shot.

We cross the road and head down the street toward the immediate care center. About a half dozen corpses stagger around in front of the entrance, and there are plenty more farther down the road.

About twenty yards from the building, we come to a stop and lift our weapons. The sound of our guns firing echoes off the surrounding buildings as the dead tumble to the ground.

"Hurry up, Bones," Tim says as she runs through the doors in the waiting area. The three of us turn and take up positions around the front of the building and wait for the approaching dead to get close enough to take down. Before any of them do, we hear gunshots inside the building.

Tim looks at me, then he turns and jerks his head to tell Elise to go inside and cover her. She turns and runs through the doors while Tim and I focus our rifles on the dead.

"Nice and easy," Tim says and then he pulls the trigger. "Slow is smooth. Smooth is fast."

I point my rifle at the closest target. It's a dead guy dressed like he just came from a tennis match in the sewer. I take my time and line up my shot, breathe, and fire. He falls on the snow.

Then I focus on the woman behind him in a hot pink sports bra and spandex shorts. I take a breath and then I squeeze the trigger. The bullet does the job. Usually, I would be firing faster and probably still not killed the first guy.

"Slow is smooth," I say.

Tim fires again beside me. He turns and looks over his shoulder and then he watches while I take out another one.

"Smooth is fast," he says.

"Let's go!" Elise yells as she runs toward the exit of the clinic carrying a loaded backpack. Bones races out behind her and Tim grabs one of the bags from her so she can run faster.

We hustle up the road toward the hardware store. I shoulder my rifle and switch to my pistol because I've learned from experience that it's much easier to handle when the dead get too close and we are on the move.

Now the dead are beginning to shamble out of the alleys, side streets, and swarm the main road around us. I cover the left side of the street, remembering to be deliberate and patient when I take aim. It's much harder to do while I'm sprinting as fast as I can in the snow.

A woman with an enormous purse strangling her neck gets too close. I wait until Bones swerves to avoid her and then I take the shot.

"Not that slow," Tim yells, then he expels three corpses in rapid succession.

We get across the parking lot and Elise directs Bones to start climbing up first. Bones grabs onto the rope and grimaces as she pulls herself off the ground. When I turn around to check the parking lot behind us, I see a long line of corpses heading straight for us through the snow.

"Hurry up!" Elise yells at Bones.

"I am!" Bones yells back.

I holster my pistol to switch back to the rifle, but Elise hands me the rope and tells me to go. Bones isn't even halfway up the side of the building when I grab the rope and start to climb behind her.

My cold hands burn from the friction of gripping the rope. I pull myself up as fast as I can while I close my eyes and try not to look how far I have to go. I'm afraid I will feel like I can't make it to the top if I look at how far away it is. I just hear the sound of gunshots below me and then Tim yelling for us to hurry up.

"Blake," Bones yells.

I open my eyes and see her leaning over the edge of the roof and reaching down to help pull me over the ledge of the building. Once I get up there, I turn and take a look down.

Elise is about halfway up the rope, but Tim is still on the ground taking shots at the dead. However, they are closing in faster than he can take them down. I reach for my rifle and lean over the edge of the building.

"We need to cover them!" I say to Bones.

Tim grabs the rope and starts to climb with the dead less than twenty feet away. I start shooting at the closest ones and then here the sound of Bones pistol blasting away beside me. The bullets zip past Tim as he pulls himself and he looks up to see us pointing our guns in his direction.

"Don't shoot me goddamnit!" he yells.

Slow is smooth. Smooth is fast.

My finger pulls the trigger, and the bullet hits the rotting face of corpse that is staring up at me.

Elise reaches the top and I stop shooting to help pull her up. Except when she reaches for the ledge her fingers slip on the wet surface and then she screams as she falls off the building.

I stare at the spot she was a moment ago in disbelief. Then I glance at Bones and we both lean over the edge of the building to look down. I am surprised to find that Elise didn't end up falling to the ground. She is hanging on to Tim as he desperately clings to the rope. The pair of them dangle just a few inches above the outstretched arms of the dead.

Elise reaches up and grabs the rope above Tim's head and pulls herself up so he doesn't have to support her weight and then she starts to climb again. Both of them are gritting their teeth and glancing down in terror at the dead below as they dig deep to find the strength to pull themselves up the rope.

Finally, Elise reaches the top again. Bones and I reach down to grab her arms and help pull her over the edge. She collapses onto the snow on the roof and stares up at the sky while she gasps for air.

Tim reaches the top and we help him up, too. Then we all stand up there for a moment and stare down at the ravenous horde below while we catch our breath.

"Told you," says Tim and he pats me on the chest with the back of his hand. "Piece of cake."

CHAPTER NINETEEN

By the next morning, the dead outside have mostly wandered away from the loading dock and the snow quickly melts beneath the warmth of the sun.

"Let's go home," Tim says before he pulls open the loading bay door beside where the trailer is parked and rushes outside, firing his pistol at a pair of corpses lingering beside the semi. No point in trying to keep the noise down now since we're going to be rumbling out in that truck in a moment anyway. After Elise and Bones step through the doorway, I reach up and pull the garage door back down but stop just before it closes.

"Stich," I yell.

He growls and retreats a few steps from the door into the dark stock-room. I'm still relieved that nothing happened to him the other day, but it didn't take long for him to be annoying again.

"Come on, you shithead!" I yell at him and then he suddenly darts forward and leaps off the loading bay platform.

I yank the door all the way down and turn back to run toward the truck. Tim stands by the open door. Beside him, Elise scoops up Stitch and hands him up to Bones who disappears inside the cab. Tim fires the pistol several more times.

"Let's go," he yells. It probably isn't directed at anyone in particular, but it feels like it is directed at me.

I grab the door handle and haul myself up behind the steering wheel and then scramble back into the crowded sleeper of the cab with Bones and Stitch. The dog pants heavily and licks my face when I crawl beside him on the bed. His mouth smells horrid from his diet of whatever leftovers we have, and God knows what he finds on his own.

Tim climbs aboard the truck and dives over to the passenger seat. Elise gets in right behind him and slams the door. The dead are already swarming the truck. The chorus of moans and the dead pounding their fists on the chassis of the truck is enough to make Elise have trouble steadying her shaking hands to plug the key into the ignition.

"Hurry, hurry," Bones urges her.

Finally, she turns the engine over and the whole cab vibrates when the truck comes alive.

"Go! Go! Go!" Tim says.

The semi lurches forward suddenly and plows into the corpses blocking our way. I lose sight of them a moment later as they fall to the ground and are crushed beneath the massive truck tires. Elise accelerates down the back alley, shifting the gears as she runs over one body after another. She slows down as she rounds the back corner of the building, then hits the gas again as the truck splashes through the huge puddles in the parking lot that were left by the melting snow.

Maybe we're not out of the woods just yet, but it feels relatively safe in the powerful truck. Elise smashes into another one of the things, and at this speed the decayed body just explodes from the impact. Bone fragments and gore shower the windshield. None of us can help but express our disgust with our own groans. Elise turns on the wipers and sprays the blackened muck with washer fluid that smears it around.

"Fucking hell," says Bones.

Elise gags. Her cheeks puff out and she puckers her lips tightly and covers her mouth.

"Watch the road," Tim urges here. He reaches across to grab the wheel, but she stops covering her lips and swats his hand away.

"I got it," she tells him.

She steers us on to the road and then takes a left back through the residential neighborhood. Elise takes her time, weaving through the abandoned vehicles and debris in the road now. When we make it back to the highway, I lean back on the small bed and let out a deep breath and just stare up at the ceiling of the truck and feel the motion of powerful machine driving us forward.

I should probably feel relieved that we made it out of Pueblo alive. Maybe I should feel grateful to Tim for saving my life, or thankful that Stitch somehow survived and all that. Even though I know I should feel these things, I don't really feel much of anything at all. I just feel this emptiness inside me like a black hole in my chest. That's all there is anymore.

I hear everyone else talking. Their voices sound hopeful and I am sort of thankful their words are drowned out by the loud engine and the sound of the tires rumbling over the highway. I just keep my eyes closed until the truck comes to a stop again. Elise shuts off the engine and I sit up and rub my eyes. I must have fallen asleep for a while.

No one moves or says anything. Everyone just stares at the empty spot where the truck the others took was parked, but now there is just a pair of tire tracks pressing down the brush.

"Doesn't mean anything," Elise says.

"No," Tim says in a flat voice that isn't at all reassuring. "It doesn't."

This is the moment where I feel like I should say something. But the truth is, I have a bad feeling too.

"It's only been a few days," Bones says. "It's—"

"Let's just get home," Tim says. He opens the truck and hops down onto the soggy grass with a dull thud. His eyes just linger on the patch of grass, and he clenches his jaw while he waits for us to get out of the truck and grab our weapons and bags.

We start the long hike up the mountain in silence except for the occasional twig snapping beneath our boots. Stitch trots ahead of us, stopping to sniff the dirt every few feet take in his surroundings. But the rest of us just stare down at the dirt as we walk. The bright sun might be shining in the afternoon sky above us, but it still feels like there is a dark cloud over all of us. Day after day, that is what life has become now. Maybe the others don't feel it yet, but it seems inevitable that they will.

We finally reach the lake and see the cabin on the distant shore. A trickle of smoke drifts up from the chimney. The sight of it does bring me at least a small amount of comfort. Not everything is lost.

The door creaks open as we approach, and Stacy emerges with the baby in her arms. She runs down the steps in her bare feet to meet Tim and wraps her arm around him.

"Hey babe," he says and kisses his wife on the head. "You okay?"

"I'm okay," she assures him. "Just tired. I hardly had any sleep at all. I was so worried."

"Nothing to be worried about," Tim lies. "We were never in any danger. I was deployed for months, and you never worried before. You know nothing could keep me from coming back to you."

"It's not that," she tells him.

"Let me hold him," Tim says.

Tim lets his bag fall to the ground. The sight of his wife and child brings a smile to Tim's face in spite of everything. He takes the baby from her and bounces him gently in his arms when the baby starts to cry.

"Shh, easy," Tim says.

I glance toward the open door.

"Where's Amanda?" I ask.

Stacy stares at me for a moment with her mouth open and I already know that whatever happened is not going to be good.

"She's inside," Stacy says.

"What happened?" I ask her. "What's wrong?"

I walk towards the door without even waiting for an answer.

"Wait," Stacy says. "Blake!"

But I am already running up the steps.

"Stacy," I hear Bones say. "Tell me what's going on?"

I push through the front door and look around at the empty furniture and the crackling fireplace. Then I rush down the hallway and open the door to the bedroom.

I can barely discern a body lying in the bed from the fading daylight coming through the window. I want to throw on the light switch, but I am afraid of what I will see if I do. Instead, I stare at the motionless shape in the darkness and hold my breath and wait for something to happen. Each second that goes by while nothing happens feels like an eternity.

"Amanda," I whisper.

When she doesn't say anything back, I feel my legs start to go numb. I feel light-headed and I barely make it a few feet to the side of the bed before I drop to my knees. It seems like a cruel twist of fate that I would find her again only to have all this happen.

Bones hurries into the room and brushes past me. She reaches down and places a hand on Amanda's neck. She pulls a pen light from her pocket and clicks it on and uses a finger to pry open Amanda's eyelid and shine the light on her fixated brown eyes. That's when I realize she might actually still be alive.

"Is she—" I begin to say but can't manage to finish the sentence.

"Blake," Bones says. "I need a minute, please."

"What's wrong with her?" I demand.

She ignores me and digs around in her bag and curses under her breath. Bones removes a stethoscope and puts the metal circle on her belly and listens.

I watch in silent horror until I feel like I really must have lost my mind and maybe this is all just some terrible delusional nightmare that I am trapped inside forever. The tears start to well up in my eyes and I feel close to losing control.

"Please," I beg her.

She holds a finger to shush me and listens a bit more.

"She is in a coma," Bones tells me.

"A coma," I say. "How?"

"I think something is wrong with the baby," she says.

CHAPTER TWENTY

Steam rises from a bowl of yellowish broth that sits untouched on the kitchen table. I stare at it and try to wrap my mind around everything that is happening.

"She just collapsed," says Stacy. "She started convulsing."

"Like a seizure?" Bones asks.

"Yeah," Stacy says. "I'm sorry. I didn't know what to do for her."

"You did fine," Bones assures her.

"So, what's wrong with her?" Tim asks.

"It sounds like eclampsia maybe," Bones says. "I don't know. This isn't really my area of expertise. I'm just guessing."

"If you're right, what does that mean?" Tim says.

"I don't know," Bones sighs and rests her forehead in her palm and stares down at the wooden grain of the kitchen table and thinks for a moment."

"Is she going to live?" I finally ask.

"Her blood pressure is really high," Bones says. "I'm afraid we might have to make a choice," she says.

"A choice?" I say. "What choice."

"If she carries this baby, she could have a stroke. There is a good chance it could kill her. Even then, there is no guarantee the baby will survive. If you want to save Amanda, the best chance to do that is to terminate the pregnancy."

"Terminate?" I say.

"Shit," Tim curses. Stacy brings a clenched fist up to her lips and starts to cry. She buries her face in Tim's chest.

"I'm sorry," Bones says to me.

"It's not even mine," I say. "How can I choose?"

It seems like a strange thought to have at that moment, but I can't help thinking it. I really don't know what I should do. I have no idea what Amanda would want me to decide.

"I can't," I say. "I can't make that choice. I won't."

"Someone has to," Bones tells me.

Silence descends on the room and even though I am holding my head in my hands and staring down at the table, I feel the eyes of everyone else in the room upon me and the growing weight of the silence compounding each second that I say nothing.

"We don't have time—" Bones begins, but then I interrupt her.

"Do it," I whisper.

"Are you sure?" Bones says softly.

I look up and glance around the table. My eyes pause on Stacy. She holds the baby in her arms and bounces him gently as he sleeps. She averts her eyes and stares down at her baby to avoid eye contact. After taking a deep breath, I look at Bones and silently bow my head to let her know I'm not going to change my mind.

"I'm sure," I say.

She turns toward Elise.

"Give me a hand?" she asks.

Elise hesitates for a moment and then reluctantly nods her head. The two of them leave the kitchen and head down the hall to the bedroom.

The baby lets out a sudden cry. Stacy cradles the boy against her chest and hushes it. I don't know if she senses the sound will be upsetting right now or if she is feeling emotional about the situation, but she rushes out of the kitchen. The cries of the baby trail off until I hear the bedroom door close, and the house falls silent again.

Tim leans back against the kitchen counter and folds his arms across his chest. He stares down at the floor with his mouth open, like he is searching between the cracks of the planks for the right thing to say.

"Look…" he says. "For what it's worth, you—"

I raise my hand to get him to stop talking. It's not that I don't appreciate the concern, but there isn't really anything to say about it that's going to make it any easier to live with.

"It's okay," I tell him. "I appreciate it. But it is what it is."

Tim uncrosses his arms and presses lips tightly together. He pushes his body away from the counter and then shoves his hands into his pockets and leaves me alone in the kitchen.

I stare down at the soup listening to the sound of the freezing wind blowing against the house.

It seems like I should feel upset or sad right now, or at least that I should feel something, but the only thing I feel is exhaustion. It isn't the kind of exhaustion that any amount of sleep will fix. This is something entirely different. Any hope I had has been gone for a while and there is nothing left to feel love or sadness or anything else.

That made this decision easier. I do hope that Amanda will be okay. I don't want to lose her. Nothing else matters beyond that. I'd be lying if I felt some emotions over the loss of the baby. Maybe that makes me a monster, but the world is full of monsters now. There is no future. Not anymore.

No more warming steam rises from the bowl in front of me. Reluctantly, I pick up the spoon and stir the liquid around then let the spoon fall from my fingers and clang against the ceramic rim. I push the bowl away from me and lean back and stare up at the ceiling and listen to the howling wind some more.

Eventually, my stomach gurgles and then I stare at the cold soup still sitting on the table. I pull it back towards me and pick up the tarnished spoon and scoop some of the cold and unsatisfying broth into my mouth. There isn't anything enjoyable about eating. It is just about survival now.

I wipe the last drips from lips just before a bedroom door opens down the hall. I lift my head and see Bones standing in the doorway and wiping her hands clean with a rag. Flecks of blood spot the fabric.

"It's done," Bones says.

I don't really know what to say so I just sit there and stare at her.

"Her blood pressure is already falling. I think she'll be okay," she tells me.

"Thanks," I manage to say finally.

"Can't say I'll be okay for sure though," Bones says. "That was not really something I imagined I'd ever have to do."

She roughs the sweat off her brow with her forearm and then tries to smile even though I can tell by her watery eyes that she can barely keep it together right now.

"I'm sorry you had to do it," I say. "But I am glad that you were here to do it."

"We just do what we have to do," she says. "Right?"

"Yeah," I say.

She sniffs and then nods her head quickly in agreement as she glances down at her shoes. I notice there are some drops of blood on them also. Her eyes lock on them for a long moment.

"Just give me another minute to clean up," Bones tells me. "She is still unconscious, but you can sit with her if you want to."

"Sure," I say.

While I wait, I get up and put the bowl in the sink. While the water runs and rinses out the bowl, I stare out the kitchen window into the dark night. Leaves flutter through the air and tree branches thrash back in forth as a cold rain starts to fall.

With everything going on I hadn't even had much chance to think about Scout and Fletcher. It's been days without any word from them at all. I hope they're okay even though I know damn well by now that none of us are ever really okay anymore. I can't help but feel like something bad has probably happened to them. It seems like there is always something bad happening now.

I leave the window and head to the bedroom. In the doorway, I pause for a moment and wait while Bones covers Amanda with a blanket and grabs her medical bag off the floor. I turn my body to make room for her to get through the doorway, but she pauses for a moment next to me and glances back at Amanda in the bed.

"Talk to her," she tells me. "Even if she isn't conscious, she will still recognize your voice. It might help."

"Okay," I say.

After she leaves me alone in the room, I remain in the doorway for a long time and just stare at her lying in the bed. Finally, I step to the side of the bed and settle into the wooden chair situated beside her. I'm not really sure what to say and my mouth feels dry, so I just reach out and hold her hand for a moment. All I can think about is how different it feels. Her hands are not soft anymore, but tough and hard. Her fingers are bony and the fingernails she used to have manicured are chipped and chewed and have bits of dirt and grime beneath that seems like it never comes off with soap and water.

"Amanda," I finally say to her softly that even I can hardly hear the words over the howling wind outside.

Even though I know she can't respond, I still stop speaking for a moment because I don't know what there is to say really. Her eyes are closed, and her body is still except for the almost imperceptible rise and fall of her chest while she breathes.

"I know this won't be easy," I say. "And I'm sorry for that. I hope you will find a way to forgive me. Not sure I deserve that. I haven't exactly been good to you lately. I've been kind of terrible if I'm being honest, I guess."

For some reason, it feels easy to talk to her right now. Maybe because I know that she won't respond. I can finally say the things that have been too hard to say.

"You know," I say. "After losing Abby, I just kept wishing I had done something more to get to her faster and save her. Now I see that maybe it was better that way. Maybe that was lucky after all. The world is ending. We aren't coming back from this. Her life would have been a fate worse than death. I hope you will understand. That's why I did what I did."

Floorboards creak behind me and I glance back over my shoulder to see Tim walking behind me in the hallway. I'm not sure how long he may have been there or what he heard but it makes me feel awkward to be heard talking to Amanda so openly by someone I don't really know all that well. I slowly place her hand back down on the bed and stare at her face for a long moment.

"Even if you can't forgive me for this," I continue. "I guess that will be okay. At least you will still be here with me for a while longer. For as long as we got left anyway. That's all that matters now."

Stitch starts barking his head off in the other room suddenly. At first, I think it is just the dog barking at the wind like a stupid asshole, but then I hear the sound of Tim slapping a magazine into a weapon and I know that something is happening. I leave Amanda and head back down the hall toward the front door. When I get to the foyer, Tim is leaning against the front door, peering through the transom into the dark night.

"There's someone out there," he whispers. "Grab a weapon."

CHAPTER TWENTY-ONE

With the gun in my hands, I watch Tim as he scans the woods outside the cabin. Stitch lets out another bark even though I already told him to shut up, so I pick up a shoe from the collection of footwear on a rug near the door and chuck it at him so that he scurries a few feet away and stares at me with a look of confusion.

"Maybe it's Fletcher," I suggest.

"No," he says. "Fletcher would know better to creep up on us in the dark without giving us a sign it was him."

"Is it the dead?"

I turn my head to see Elise and Bones standing just behind me at the end of the hallway. Elise is armed with her SMG and Bones grips a pistol tightly in her hand.

"Don't know," Tim says. "I can't see shit. Get the lights."

Elise reaches for a switch on the wall and flicks it and the lights in the family room and hallway turn off.

"Maybe it was just the wind," I say.

Tim glances outside in one direction and the other.

"No there is something out there," he says again.

I'm not really sure how he can tell this, but he seems pretty convinced.

"What do you want to do?" I say.

"We have to go out there," he says. "You ready?"

Even though I am not feeling ready for what might happen next at all, I give him a thumbs up to let him know I will be right with them when the door opens.

Tim turns the handle and pushes the door open a few inches and slides the barrel of the rifle out ahead of him. We crouch down step over the creaking floorboards and down the pair of steps and take cover behind a huge stack of firewood a few yards from the porch.

The wind gusts again and the tree branches crack and rattle in the darkness. I lift my head just enough to peer over the top of the wood pile because I can't help feeling like at any moment there will be a muzzle flash in the darkness followed by a bullet that will take the top of my head off.

Stitch trots out behind us. He continues out into the yard and casually sniffs the air as he lifts his leg and pisses on a tree stump. Maybe it was just the wind after all. That dog just has us all spooked over nothing.

Stitch slowly lowers his leg. His ears perk up and he looks back at us and barks once, low and quiet, before he turns and heads towards the trail down the mountain again.

"Over there," Tim whispers. Slow and silent, he rises and points at a shape that I mistook for a boulder on the ground in the dark. Tim clicks on a flashlight and shines the beam into the woods. "What is that?"

We all come out from behind cover and head slowly in the direction of the shape on the ground. The wind settles for a moment, and I hear labored breathing followed by a weak groan. A pair of eyes blink from the shadows when the figure moves.

"Army!" Elise yells and then she sprints ahead of us to get to him.

A series of thoughts flash through my mind as I break into a run. First, it's a sense of relief to see him alive at all. That is followed by a growing concern as I look around the woods and realize he is alone out here and seemingly hurt. Lastly, a sense of dread settles in and I am afraid to hear what he is going to say when we ask him what happened to Scout and Fletcher.

We crouch down beside the big man who shields his eyes from the flashlight. His face is filthy and covered in scrapes and crusted blood. It looks like there is a serious wound to his arm, probably a gunshot wound, but I'm just guessing in the dark.

"Armando," Bones says.

He just groans in response.

"We need to get him inside," Bones says.

"Help me move him," Tim says.

Tim and I manage to pull the big man to his feet and drape his arms across our shoulder and haul him to the house. His feet drag over the ground as he stumbles along, barely able to help keep himself upright. My legs tremble from supporting the weight of him and by the time we get through the front door and drop him onto the couch in the family room, the strain on my back causes me to wince from the pain.

"Look at me, Armando," Bones says.

He blinks his eyes again and then they roll back into his head. Bones checks his arm and then quickly looks for any other visible injuries. She looks confused for a moment, as though she can't quite figure out how to fix him.

"The arm looks like a gunshot wound," Elise says.

"It is," she says. "But it appears to be a superficial wound."

"Maybe he lost a lot of blood," Tim says.

Bones brushes the bangs off her forehead with her wrist and examines the wound.

Suddenly, his eyelids flick open again. Elise lets out a cry of terror. I take a step back and gasp for a moment until he inhales deeply and blinks his eyes several times as though to try and focus them. He grabs the backrest of the couch suddenly and tries to sit up.

"Armando," Bones says. "Take it easy." She places a hand on his chest and eases him back down until his head settles on the armrest.

"Are you okay?" she asks him.

"Mountain..." he pants. "Too much."

Army is still sucking wind and barely able to speak so he just nods his head. I'm not really sure but it seems like the hike up the mountain is the biggest reason he had collapsed in the woods instead of his other injuries.

"Let me get my bag. Then I'll take a look at your arm."

Bones gets up to her feet again.

"Stay put," she points a bloody finger at him to warn him she means it before leaving the room.

"Army," Tim says. "Where is Chuck?"

Army hesitates, his eyes stare down at his shirt for just a second but it's long enough to tell Tim that he isn't about to like what he is going to hear.

"What happened out there?" Tim says.

"I lost them," Army finally says.

"Lost them?" Tim says. He turns his back on Army for a moment and tilts his head back and stares at the ceiling. After he takes a deep breath, he turns back around. "Are they alive or not, Army?"

"Maybe," he says. "I don't know."

"Jeez—" Tim snaps.

"Tell us everything that happened," I say. "From the beginning."

"We found the kid," Army says. "We saw him at least."

"Stevie?" I say. "He's okay?"

"Well, he's alive," Army says.

"Where?"

"Exactly where she said," Army says and raises his hand to gesture towards Bones as she returns to the room. "Bishop Castle."

The name Bishop makes me immediately remember that lunatic back in Missouri. It seems unlikely, but I start to wonder if there is some kind of connection between the two. Maybe it is just random. Sometimes there are reasons for coincidences and sometimes it just feels like it. Either way, the name of this place doesn't make me want to go there.

"That's where La Parca is too," Bones says.

"Did you see him?" Tim asks Army.

"No," Army says. "But that place is a fortress. Guards everywhere. So, I think it's safe to assume that's where he is at."

He stops to clear his throat.

"Water?" Bones says.

"I'm good," Army tells her.

"So, what went down there?" Tim says.

"When we got there and saw what it looked like, Fletcher knew we were in over our heads. So, we were just going to scope it out from a distance. Once we spotted the kid, Scout made up her mind that she was going to get him out of there by any means necessary. You know how she gets."

Army stops for a moment and glances around the room.

"That's when it started snowing like crazy. Chuck thought we could maybe slip in late at night without being noticed. I knew it was *loco*. I'm too big to sneak in anywhere without being noticed. It almost worked, though."

"Almost?" Tim says.

"We made it inside," Army says. "But then we walked right by these *Cholos.* I knew it was not good the way they were eyeing us. One of them gestured toward me and said whisper something about *la prisión.*

"You think they recognized you from the prison?" Tim asks.

"I think so," Army says. "When they started following us, I knew what was about to go down, but by that time there was no going back. Chuck told Scout to let us handle them and go find the kid and then get the hell out of there. That was the last time we saw her."

"What happened next?" Tim says.

"Chuck wanted to just play it cool," Army says. "He lit a joint and smoked it and waited for them to walk up to us. Those homies weren't buying it. They came up on us with their guns and I could tell it was about to get messy. A second later the shooting started, but it wasn't us. There was someone else there."

"Someone else?" I say.

"They saved our asses. I didn't get a look at them, but someone cut down those motherfuckers and it wasn't us. At first, I thought maybe it was you."

Tim and I exchange looks of confusion.

"After that," Army says. "Bullets started flying everywhere, homie. We scrambled to find some cover. I tried to stay with Chuck but then I got tagged and dropped my gun in the snow when I went down. Then I ducked behind a shed for cover. I looked around but there was no sign of him. There were people shouting in all directions, bullets flying. It was a blizzard by then too and there was the dragon on the castle shooting fire into the sky."

"The what?" I say.

"Dragon," he repeats.

That's what I thought he said. Hearing it twice still doesn't make it make sense.

"It's a machine," Bones tells me. "A robot."

"I didn't want to leave them there, but I didn't know what else to do," Army says. "I was bleeding. I had no weapon. I ran like a fucking coward."

The big man clenches his fingers into a fist then and hammers the cushion on the back of the couch.

"I'm fucking sorry," he says. "I got back to the trees and waited for twenty minutes until the shooting finally stopped. I didn't know what else to do, so I hiked back to the truck and waited but they never came back. I should have done something."

"Easy," Tim tells him. "That's not on you. Chuck knew damn well what he was getting himself into going in there. You got out of there alive and made it back here. That's the best thing you could do under the circumstances."

"Do you think there is any chance they could still be alive?" Elise asks him.

"I don't know," Army says.

I can't really tell if he is uncertain or if he is just afraid to admit that in all likelihood both Scout and Fletcher are already dead. Either way, a solemn silence takes over the room. Tim walks to the recliner in the far corner and slowly settles down into the seat. He stares at one of the pictures on the wall beside him. It is a black and white photo of him and his brother in their fatigues, both smiling in front of a military helicopter.

"What do you want to do, Tim?" Elise says.

Tim digs his fingertips into the armrest cushions of the chair and stares at the picture as though he cannot hear a word she says until there is a loud knock at the front door.

CHAPTER
TWENTY-TWO

S titch growls softly at the door but hushes when I wave my hand at him. All eyes in the room stare at the front door. I adjust my grip on the rifle and glance back at Tim easing himself up from the chair.

"Someone must have followed him," Tim whispers before holding a finger to his lips as he creeps over to the couch to retrieve the rifle leaning against the wall beside it.

There is another knock on the door. This time it is much faster and more forceful. Whoever is out there isn't very patient. They also aren't afraid of us at all. It's the end of the world. Nobody just stops by and knocks on your door anymore.

The doorknob jiggles but it is locked and deadbolted.

"Open up," says a man outside. The howling wind and rain pattering on the rooftop drown out his voice, so he seems to be farther away than he actually is.

There is a long pause. Tim switches off the safety on his weapon and levels it at the door.

"I know you're hurt," the man says. "I can help."

Another pause. The voice doesn't really sound very sincere, but there is something familiar about it all the same. Whoever he is, he seems to think that Army is alone in here. It also sounds like he might be by himself as well.

"It's okay," the man says. "I know you don't know me, but I know that guy, Fletcher. The one you were with—"

At the mention of his brother's name Tim reaches out and flips the locks and flings the door open. The gusting wind blows it back so that it slams against the wall so loudly that, for a second, I thought someone started shooting. Tim keeps the rifle ready at his shoulder and pointed out into the night. From my angle, I can't see who is outside in the darkness.

"Who the fuck are you?" the man says to Tim. There is something very familiar about the voice. I know I have heard him before.

"Hands up," Tim warns him.

Stitch starts barking again and runs to the door.

"Keep them where I can see them," Tim says.

"Hey, I know that little fucking dog," says the man.

I walk toward the door then and Chase looks up from beneath the soaking wet hood of his sweatshirt and locks eyes with me.

"Shit," he mutters in a voice that could be shock, disappointment, or both.

Not the way most people greet me, but I guess I have to kind of expect it coming from Chase. I did nearly shoot him after all.

"You know this guy?" Tim asks me.

"Yeah," I say. "I know him."

Since this started, I lost so many people that meant a lot to me. Chase was not one of them. I am not at all excited to see him again.

Tim lowers the rifle but looks Chase over again for a long moment and lingers in the doorway.

"You going to let me in or make stand out here in the goddamn rain all night?" Chase says to Tim.

Tim eventually steps aside to allow him to come inside. Chase glances around the room at the faces of everyone else in the room.

"You said you know my brother," Tim says.

"Brother?" Chase says. "Fletcher? He's your brother?"

"Yeah," Tim says. "You know what happened to him?"

"No," Chase says. "If I had to guess, I'd say he probably bought it back there, but I've been wrong about that before."

Tim furrows his brow in what seems like a mix of concern and confusion, but I know that Chase is referring to leaving Chuck behind in that hotel.

"Yes, you were, Chase," I say.

"I didn't think you'd forget about that either," he nods. "Okay."

"Feels like I'm missing an important piece of information in this conversation," Tim says.

"You had to be there," Chase tells him before he shrugs off his wet coat and pulls his hood off his head. His eyes search our faces and the walls of the room.

"You out there alone?" I ask him.

His eyes lock with mine again and I can tell by the anxious way he clenches his jaw that he knows what I am really asking about is Natalie.

"Yeah," he says.

"You army?" he says.

"How you know my name, homie?" Army says.

"What?" Chase says. "Your name? I wasn't even talking to you. I'm asking him."

Chase gestures toward Tim with his hand that is missing fingers.

"Yeah," Tim says. "Special Forces. You?"

"Marine," Chase says. "Recon."

That seems to be enough to settle the tension between the men slightly and Tim flips the safety back on his rifle and stows it on the rack by the wall.

"You followed him back here?" Tim asks.

"Wasn't hard," Chase says. "Kind of surprised those Reapers didn't get here first. You won't live long being careless like that."

"How are you sure nobody followed you?" Army says.

"I'm sure," Chase grins. "By the way, you're welcome. In case you didn't notice, I'm the guy that killed those gangbangers and saved your sorry ass out there."

The guy is still just as irritating as I remember.

"What were you doing there anyway?" I ask him.

"We went there looking to steal a car," Chase says. "Trying to get the hell out of here. Should have been easy. We were just waiting until dawn so that nobody was likely to notice. Then Nat spots Chuck and Scout strolling up the driveway with fat boy over there."

"What?" Army says. He pushes himself upright and Bones grabs his shoulder to keep him from trying to get to his feet. "*Pinche puto—*"

"No offense," Chase stops him. "I didn't mean nothing by it. Everybody is still so goddamn sensitive."

"Then what happened?" Tim interjects.

Chase walks across the room and collapses into the red recliner that Tim had just got out of when we heard a knock on the door. He also stares at the photos on the wall for a minute while he thinks about what he is about to say.

"I tried to tell Nat to leave it alone. It wasn't our problem, and I was done getting involved with that. She wouldn't listen, so I left her there. I figured she'd come to her senses and follow me like always. She didn't though. Soon as I heard the first shot, I knew shit was about to go sideways. I spun around and let it rip. They never knew what hit them."

His trigger finger taps lightly against the side of the pistol grip while he talks. It makes me edgy and concerned at the same time.

"A few seconds later, those motherfuckers came rushing out at us from every direction. Nat tried to bug out, but she took a bullet in the leg and couldn't run. She crawled behind a tree stump and was pinned down there. I don't know why I did it, but I went back for her." Chase says. "Even though I already knew deep down I wouldn't get her out of there alive."

Chase stops speaking for a moment and clears his throat. It's the only time I can recall that it seems like he might actually be feeling something close to emotion.

"She was losing a lot of blood," Chase says. "Somehow, she was still conscious for a minute and started mumbling something about being sorry and telling me to leave her. I was so mad at her I just told her to shut up and then her eyes rolled back in her head. That was the last thing I said to her."

Chase takes a deep breath, and his glazed-over eyes focus on the room once again and he glances around at all the faces watching him.

"I pulled her up by her arm and carried her over my shoulder and ran like hell up the goddamn hill. Several rounds hit her in the back. I heard the bullets landing. Felt all of them, too. Somehow, none of them wounded me. Kind of funny. I couldn't manage to save her, but she probably saved me."

Chase forces a little uncomfortable laughter even though none of this is funny at all. It's pretty clear it is his way of trying to avoid showing the pain he really feels. Still, I don't feel bad for him. Natalie didn't have to die. She made a bad choice when she left with him, and it ended up getting her killed.

"Her body was already getting cold when I got far enough away to stop running. I set her down against a boulder to check her wounds. Check for a pulse. But she was gone. Her cheeks were pale and blue. I didn't know where else to go then, so I just sat there for a while until I saw big boy over there stumbling through the snow. And here we are."

Chase leans back in the recliner when he finishes speaking and takes a deep breath. He glances around and then looks down at Stitch and the dog stares at him and growls quietly.

"What's his fucking problem?" Chase says. He lifts his boot off the ground suddenly and threatens to kick Stitch with it and the scruffy mutt scurries away and cowers beside my feet. For a second, I nearly started to think maybe he had changed, but now I realize the chances of that ever actually happening and minuscule.

"What are you doing here?" I ask Chase. "What do you want?"

It likely isn't hard for him to detect the animosity in my voice, but I don't really care anymore. We have plenty of reasons not to like each other at this point so there is no sense in pretending to get along.

"I got to settle up the score with those Reapers," he finally says. "Seems like we all do. As much as I don't like to ask for it, I'm going to need some help. I can't do it by myself."

"You want help from us?" I say.

"Blake," he says. "I'm not asking you to do it for me. Do it for, Natalie. Claire. Danielle. Do it for everyone else those fuckers have killed. We own them that."

CHAPTER
TWENTY-THREE

"You don't seem so sure about this guy," Tim whispers after he calls me into the kitchen to lend a hand with something. Really, I know he just wants to talk for a minute where Chase can't hear us. He holds the sleeping baby in his arms and bounces him gently.

"We don't really get along," I tell him. "Chuck told you about the hotel we left him at?"

"Yeah," says Tim.

"Chase told us he was sure Chuck was dead," I say. "That was why we never went back."

Tim stares down at the face of his child as he thinks this over then.

"You think we can't trust him then?" Tim says.

My first instinct is to tell him no, but then I think back to a couple of days ago when I lost my shit and nearly got us both killed in the street and wonder if Chase is actually a bigger liability.

"I don't know," I admit.

"If we do this, we can't afford any mistakes," Tim says.

I hear a rough scratching sound behind me. I glance over my shoulder to see Stacy violently scraping at the dirt on the counter with a sponge.

"Stacy," Tim whispers.

She stops her assault on the counter and sighs.

"You promised, Tim," Stacy says. "You said you were done with all this. You know how this ends."

"I know," Tim says. "I tried to explain it to them before, but this is the current situation. There is no avoiding it anymore."

"Sure there is," Stacy snaps. She loses her temper for a moment and raises her voice loud enough to wake the baby up. He lets out a cry and then Tim resumes bouncing him gently until Stacy tosses the dirty sponge into the sink and reaches out to take the baby off his hands.

"If Elise was—," Tim says.

"Don't!" Stacy interrupts him.

"Stacy," Tim says. "Chuck might still be alive. He might need help."

"He might," Stacy says. "He might also be dead. You know I love him too, but I can't lose you now, Tim. I can't do this on my own."

"Hey," Tim says and wraps an arm around her. "You know there is nothing that can keep me from coming back to you."

He kisses her on the head and pulls her close to him. I feel awkward standing there in the kitchen, so I nervously shift my weight from one foot to the other.

"When are you leaving?" Stacy asks.

"We need to go now," he says.

"Now?" she says. "It's the middle of the night."

"We already sat around here long enough as it is," Tim says.

"Every minute we lose sitting here decreases the odds of finding any of them alive," I say.

"Right," says Tim. He releases his wife from his embrace and looks into her eyes once more. "Be back before you even have time to miss me."

"I already miss you," she says.

He gives her one more kiss.

"Let's get going," he says to me.

We return to the family room once again. Tim glances around the faces in the room for a moment. I can tell he is still reluctant to leave his home and put any other lives at risk.

"What's the word?" Chase asks. "We going to kick some ass or what?"

"I can't really speak for anyone else, but I'm on board," Tim tells him.

"Glad the old lady gave you permission," Chase says.

Tim ignores the comment and instead looks at Army. The big man sits up on the couch.

"I'm coming," he says.

"I don't think that's a good idea," Bones says.

"You sure you're up for it?" Tim asks.

"Just give him a couple painkillers or something," Chase says. "He's a big boy."

"I'll be fine," Army insists.

"Count me in, too," Elise says.

"Elise, I was going to ask you to stay behind on this one," Tim says.

"What?" Elise says. "Why?"

"Stacy can use a hand here with the baby," he says.

"I'll help her," Bones says. "I'm not going. Amanda isn't out of the woods just yet. So, I can lend Stacy a hand, too."

"Okay," says Tim. "If we're going to do this we need to go now, so everyone else grab what you need and let's get moving."

Chase jumps up from the recliner and pulls the hood of his damp sweatshirt back over his head.

"You got some kind of plan?" I ask Tim.

"There isn't time for plans," Tim says.

"I don't suppose you got a stockpile of weapons or ammunition sitting around," Chase says.

"We'll get you straightened out," Tim says him.

"I need a minute," I tell Tim.

"Hurry up," he says.

I walk back down the hall and return to the bedroom where Amanda is lying on the bed. I linger in the doorway and stare at her peaceful face for a moment until Bones appears behind me and squeezes through the door beside me to get to the bed. She checks Amanda for a pulse and then wraps a cuff around her arm and pumps it full of air.

"How is she doing?" I ask Bones.

"Better," Bones says. "I'll keep a close eye on her still, but I think she will be okay soon."

She peels apart the Velcro on the cuff and it makes a tearing sound that seems incredibly loud in the relative quiet of the bedroom.

"Don't worry," she assures me.

"Thanks, Bones," I tell her.

She starts to leave the room, but before she walks through the door, I think of something else that is on my mind.

"Hey," I say without turning around to look at her. I just keep staring at Amanda and wondering how she will react to all this when she realizes what happened. "One more thing."

"What?" Bones says.

"If she comes out of this while I am gone, what will you tell her?" I ask.

Bones thinks about it for a second before she answers.

"The truth," she says. "I think that's what she'll want to hear."

"Right," I agree.

"Take care out there, Blake," she says.

After Bones leaves the room, I stand there beside the bed and reach out and hold her hand again once more before I have to leave. Stitch trots into the room and hops up on the bed and curls up on her lap.

I really don't want to leave her right now, but part of me is also afraid to be here when she first wakes up and finds out what has happened. Deep down, I know that things are already so complicated between us. It seems like this will certainly make it even worse. At least she is still alive. Right now, it feels like that is all I have left anymore.

"I'll be back soon," I tell her, and then I bend down and kiss her on the forehead.

As much as I feel guilty about it, I let go of her hand and leave the room. I get to the door and wait for Stitch, but he is still curled up on Amanda's lap.

"You coming?" I ask him.

He opens his eyes and lifts his head. Stitch stares at me and yawns and then rests his head on Amanda again. I guess he is staying here with her. It seems silly, but it makes me feel better that she will have him with her right now.

The others have their coats on and are waiting on the front porch. Their breath drifts toward the sky in clouds that catch the moonlight. I grab my coat hanging off the rack on the wall by the front door and grab my backpack and assault rifle up off the floor.

"Here," Stacy says when I start to reach for the handle on the front door.

I turn around and take what she is holding out for me and stare down at it with a confused expression on my face. It's something cold concealed in a layer of tinfoil.

"Thanks," I say, even though I'm not really sure what she is giving me.

"It's just jerky," she tells me. "Sorry."

"It's all good," I tell her. "I appreciate it, Stacy."

I turn to leave again but she grabs my arm to keep me from opening the door again.

"Blake," she says. "I can tell you're a rational guy. Watch out for Elise and Tim. Try not to let them do anything too risky. I don't know what I'd do without them."

I look into her eyes and see the fear and uncertainty she feels. The truth is I haven't been very rational at all lately. If anything, I was the one that was distressed and endangering us out there. But telling her that won't make her feel any better.

"Of course," I say. "I'll do my best."

She lets go of my arm and smiles to show her appreciation. I tuck the food into my back and step out onto the porch pulling the door closed behind me. The night air sends a chill through my body that causes me to shiver immediately.

"Everything good?" Tim asks.

"Yeah," I say. "Good."

"What did Stacy need?" he says.

"Just had some food for us," I lie. "Jerky."

Tim looks back at the front of the cabin one more time and waves at Stacy who is still staring out the window. She slowly holds up a hand and leaves it up in the air.

"Let's get moving," Tim says and clicks on a flashlight. It seems to take much effort for him to turn his head and take those first few steps toward the trail down the mountain.

I'm not really sure what time it is right now. So much has happened that this night feels like it has lasted at least a week. My best guess is that it must be about three or four in the morning. Somewhere in the tree branches above us an owl hoots.

The wind kicks up a flurry of leaves that flutter around our legs as we walk. I zip up my jacket to try and stay warm as we make our way down towards the base of the mountain.

"I hate this fucking cold," Chase says.'

"Just wait until winter," Tim tells him. "This ain't nothing."

"Don't understand how people can live like this," Chase says.

"You get used to it," Tim says. "Then it doesn't seem so bad."

"Story of my life," Chase says.

I'd be lying if I said that I was glad that Tim and Chase seem to be getting along just fine. But something does seem different about Chase. Sure, he is still an asshole. But maybe he has finally hit bottom and has figured that out. I can't really say for sure yet.

The sun is peeking over the snowcapped mountains on the horizon by the time we reach the bottom of the mountain. We walk over to the trailer and stand near the rear doors while Tim undoes the latch and opens the rear doors of the truck.

Chase whistles when he sees all the stuff loaded into the back of the truck.

"Got any .300 blackout?" Chase asks.

Tim hands him half a dozen boxes or so of ammunition.

"Where'd you guys get all this?" Chase asks.

"Pueblo," Elise says.

"Elise," Tim says. He stares at her with his lips pressed together and hands her several boxes of ammo.

"No shit?" Chase says. "Pueblo."

Tim opens another bag and pulls out a few flak jackets and hands one to Elise, one to Army, and the other one to me.

"You good?" he asks Chase.

Chase pulls the neck of his sweatshirt down to reveal the plate carrier underneath.

"I'll take some nine-mil, too," Chase says.

Tim hands him a couple boxes of nine-millimeter rounds. We continue to fill our magazines and check our load outs in silence for several minutes. Something about the quiet efficiency and redundancy of it is reassuring.

After we finish loading, Tim hops down and closes the back of the truck. The squeaky metal latches squeal loudly in the quiet morning air.

We walk toward the pair of vehicles that Army and Chase drove here. Only one has enough fuel still in the tank to get where we are going, the black Jeep Cherokee that Chase says he tactically acquired— whatever that means.

No one is talking about it, but I can feel a heightened level of tension in the air. We know what we are getting ourselves into. There is a good chance that none of us will come back alive. It doesn't bother me so much because I know from the chill in the air that winter is upon us, and our days are numbered anyway.

CHAPTER
TWENTY-FOUR

Tim reaches for the button on the dashboard and flips on the radio. Chase switches his hand on the steering wheel and takes his eyes off the road to watch Tim turning the dial from one station to the next but only gets a different frequency of static. He finally settles on one and then he turns the volume down a couple notches and sits back in his seat and stares out at the mountains in the distance.

"There's nothing on," Chase tells him.

"I know," Tim says.

Chase turns his head to glance at Tim a couple times and looks confused, but then he just returns his eyes to the road and lets it go.

The continual droning sound has a soothing numbness to it. At first my mind focuses on it, and then suddenly I am no longer thinking about that instead of all the things there are to worry about. After a few minutes, I'm not thinking about anything at all and just staring blankly at the horizon, too. The trees are dropping gold and ruby-tinted leaves from their branches. They collect the frost-covered ground that glistens in the sunlight. As ugly as the world has become, some things are still the same.

In the seat beside me, Army closes his eyes. His head lolls to one side and a few minutes later he starts to snore softly. It's been a couple of days since we've really had any sleep and all of us are exhausted.

Chase takes a left turn and heads down a small road. It winds back and forth as it navigates around the mountainside. Eventually we roll through a desolate ghost town that appears to have been abandoned for over a hundred years. The wooden buildings look like something out of an old western movie. Somehow, they're still standing even after the cities have been overrun by the dead.

Eventually, the entire world will be like this. Humans will go extinct. The dead bodies will wander the land until they finally decompose and then there is nothing else left except the remnants of the dead. The bones of buildings and men that will haunt the earth.

I turn my head to look at the road ahead of us, but instead my eyes just see Chase staring back at me in the mirror. I stare back at him for a moment before I realize he isn't looking at me, but at the road behind us. I twist around in my seat to have a look, but I don't see anything there. The vehicle slows and Chase steers onto the gravel shoulder and comes to a stop. Chase checks the side mirror once more before shifting the car to park.

"What is it?" I ask him.

"Just making sure it's safe to stop here for a minute," he says. His fingers tap at the display on the console and pull up a map. "Can't be sure if this thing is right anymore," he says. "But it looks like there is a town just up the road. Last one before the castle."

"You think we'll run into trouble there?" Tim asks. He reaches toward the dash, turns off the static on the radio, and zooms in on the map.

"Maybe," Chase says.

"We don't need to tip off Castillo that we're coming," Tim says.

"At the very least we probably don't want roll through the middle of town without scoping it out first."

"Good call," Tim agrees. He turns his head and scans our surroundings. His eyes settle on the remains of a small burned down house up the road. Even though the house is ruined, there is a detached garage that was far enough away to survive the fire.

"Pull down that driveway," Tim says. "We can stash the Jeep in that garage."

Chase shifts the car back in drive and turns down the long gravel driveway up ahead. We pull up in front of the closed garage door and then Tim opens the passenger door.

"Be right back," he says.

"I'll come with if you want," Elise says.

"I got it," Tim says. "Should just take a minute."

He leaves the door ajar when he gets out to go around to the door on the side of the garage. A chime dings every few seconds to alert us to the open door. The annoying sound makes it seem like Tim is gone for an eternity even though it is probably only a couple of minutes before the garage door slides open.

Tim steps to the right and waves us into the opposite side of the garage. Behind him, the body of a guy in soiled jeans and a bloody white t-shirt hangs from the ceiling by a rope. The dead man moves and disturbs the cobwebs that surround him.

As the vehicle pulls into the space alongside him, I notice his face is all bloated and his milky, bulging black eyes are almost coming out of his skull. The constant strain of hanging by the rope has nearly torn through his neck over many months.

The dead guy grabs at the air and snaps his teeth at me when I get out of the vehicle. The meager remaining tissue holding his frame together finally gives way. The dead body crashes to the floor and the severed head smacks on the bloody cement floor beside it. The mouth opens and closes continuously as a dark fluid from the black eyes trickles down his cheeks.

No one says anything but each of us stares at the thing on the floor in horror and disgust except for Chase. He glances at the scene as he pops open the trunk. His blank expression doesn't change as he grabs his rucksack from the back of the truck and closes the door.

"Dumb bastard should have really thought that out some more," he says.

Maybe he was a dumb bastard, but he was still human. I feel like I shouldn't have to remind myself of that. These days it gets too easy to forget.

When I look at Chase, I realize that maybe it was this way long before the world ended. Some people long ago started seeing anyone that didn't fit their view of what humanity should be as less than human. It made killing each other easier and it made it easier for the rest of us to pretend it didn't impact us. It was always as mindless and instinctive as it is now.

"Let's get moving," Tim says.

I linger there for a moment longer and stare at the hideous face until everyone else has left the garage. Then I follow them out and pull down the garage behind me.

We cross through the field and then head for a line of trees to stay out of sight of the road as we head towards the edge of the small town. The sun is shining bright today, but that air is still frigid even though it is almost noon. Other than the sound of our feet crackling the twigs on the ground, there is relentless silence all around us. The birds seem to have all migrated elsewhere. It really hits home how utterly empty the world is becoming.

"Head for that water tower," Tim says. His voice booming in comparison to the relative quiet. He gestures toward the white structure in the distance. It sits on the edge of town in a field behind a line of small ranch homes. "We can probably scope out the whole town from there."

"Seems pretty quiet," Chase says.

"I want to be sure," Tim says.

When we get to the base of the water tower, I pull out the jerky from my bag and tear off a greasy piece of the chewy meat and pass it Elise. I watch Tim climb up the ladder while I chew the same salty bite for what seems like forever.

"Thanks," Elise says.

Once he reaches the top, Tim pulls a pair of binoculars and scans the town. Elise passes the meat to Army and he grabs a giant hunk and shoves it in his mouth. Chase watches as the big man as he chews impatiently, but Army is so focused on the food that he does not seem to notice until Chase clears his throat. Army stops chewing for a moment and locks eyes with Chase.

"What?" Army says.

"Don't suppose you might be willing to share some of that with me, big guy?" Chase says.

Army just stares at him while he takes another piece of jerky and shoves it in his mouth.

"*Pssh*," Chase scoffs. He smirks and shakes his head like he isn't taking it too seriously.

"See anything?" Elise asks.

"Yeah," Tim says. He climbs back down the last few rungs of the ladder before he continues. "Looks like there is a patrol at the high school. Eight hostiles, two vehicles."

"Nothing we can't handle," Chase says.

"Hold up. We have to be careful," Tim says. "We can't just roll up there, guns blazing. I don't want to risk them getting on a radio and sending out word. We need to take them by surprise."

Tim stops and glances down at the wrapped foil that Army is holding out to him.

"What's this?" he says.

"Jerky," Army says, and tiny pieces of meat fall from his lips as he talks. "Have some."

"I'm good," Tim says and pushes it away gently.

"I'll take some then," Chase says.

Army grabs one more chunk of jerky out for himself. Then he crumbles the foil up and tosses it to Chase a little harder than necessary so that it hits him in the chest and the Marine nearly drops it on the ground.

"I guess that's the thanks I get for saving your ass," Chase says. "Ungrateful fucking—"

Army takes a step toward Chase, but Tim puts himself between the two men to keep the peace.

Chase is making as many friends as usual. I guess it's good that Tim is here to step in because I wasn't about to intervene.

"Focus," Tim says. "I know we're all tired as hell and burnt out, but this isn't the time to get sloppy. We have to keep our shit together."

Usually Tim is very calm, but even he has been through a lot the last few days and it is starting to get to him as well.

"We're good," Chase tells Tim. He peels open the aluminum foil and pinches a piece of jerky. He tosses it in his mouth while staring at Army. "Right, amigo?"

Army takes a step back and then shakes his head. I can tell he is still mad, but I think Army knows it isn't worth it.

"I'm feeling really confident that we can get this done now," I say to Tim.

He lowers his head and stares at the ground for a moment before he bends down and picks up his rucksack and rifle off the ground.

"Okay enough with all the alpha male bullshit," Elise speaks up. "How do you guys want to do this?"

Tim starts walking toward town and the rest of us trail along right behind him through the yards of ransacked houses. Bodies decompose in the overgrown grass beside weathered lawn decorations and broken patio furniture.

"We should split up," Tim suggests. "Come at them from different directions. I'll circle around the back of the school and hit them from the north. You three hit them from the south."

"I work better alone," Chase says.

"Hey, asshole," Tim stops walking and grabs a handful of the black hoodie that Chase is wearing. "You came to us for help, remember?"

Chase stares at him for a long moment before he slowly moves his mouth and smiles innocently.

"No more John Wayne bullshit," Tim says and releases his grip on Chase. "We have work to do. It's time to punch in."

CHAPTER
TWENTY-FIVE

A few minutes ago, I was mostly worried that we would not survive against our enemies. Now, I just hope we don't kill each other first.

After we cut through several yards, we emerge onto the Main Street through town. We pause for a moment in front of the open garage door of the fire department and look around.

This place is another ghost town. It doesn't seem like there was anything of value in these buildings to begin with, but it's all gone now anyway. The houses and shops are all empty aside from a dead body here and there or some discarded trash, broken glass, or worthless junk.

"What a shithole," Chase mutters.

Army glances in his direction, then looks up and down the street.

"There's nothing here," Army says. "Not even a zombie."

"Zombies," Chase says. He presses his lips together and pushes a little laugh through his nostrils.

"What?" Army says.

"It just sounds stupid," Chase says. "Zombies."

"That's what they are," says Army. He gets quiet again for a moment as he scans the street ahead of us. "It does sound pretty stupid, though."

I walk along a few steps behind Army and Chase because I am tired, but mostly because I feel like I need to keep an eye on both of them still. The tension seems to have subsided for now, but I can tell they still don't particularly like each other.

"In there," Chase says and points at an open back-alley door of a small cafe. Inside, we cover our mouths in a futile attempt to hide from the smell of rot in the kitchen. A layer of fuzzy mold grows all over the counters and the tile floors.

We move through the swinging doors to the dining room and crouch behind the brick wall beneath the front windows. The high school is a drab looking brick building just across the three-way intersection.

Three men stand around a fire burning in metal trash can near a pair of narco tanks that block the road going north to the castle. Another man sits behind a fifty-cal in the nest of the turret on the roof of the armored sport-utility vehicle.

"Got two over there," Chase whispers and points at a couple more men with rifles standing next to the sign at the entrance to the high school parking lot. One of the men scans the road to the south with a pair of binoculars while the other casually smokes a cigarette.

Tim had said he had counted eight, but I scan the area and fail to find the other two. Then we hear a gunshot. Our heads duck down behind the brick wall again as soon as we hear the noise, but it doesn't seem like the gunfire is meant for us since it didn't hit the cafe windows or the building.

We peer through the murky glass again see the other two men. They're standing near a basketball court across the other road that heads east. One man sits on a park bench drinking from a bottle in brown paper bag. The other man points his rifle at a lone corpse that wanders up the road. He takes another shot at it and curses loudly when it also misses, and his companion points at him and laughs.

"Anyone spot Tim?" I say.

We search the road for several minutes.

"There," Army finally spots him and Elise as they break from the line of trees and dash across the road on the far side of the roadblock. They crouch down and find some cover behind a burned-out car on the shoulder. These guys don't seem to even be looking at the road to the north since that leads straight to the castle. They probably assume that is the last direction that someone would come at them.

"I'll take these two," Chase whispers and gestures toward the men on the basketball court. "You guys—"

A radio beeps and then there is a hiss of static in the kitchen behind us and Chase stops in middle of his sentence. Tim must not have accounted for all of them.

"You guys find something or are you just fucking around in there?" The radio squawks so loud that the speaker clips and distorts the voice of the man on the other end. "What's taking so long?"

"Turn that fucking thing down, Angel," I hear a man say in the kitchen.

"Same some for the rest of us, Pacho," says another man on the radio.

The sound of laughter and static echoes of the surfaces in the kitchen and then the radio beeps and goes silent again.

Chase pulls out a knife and silently scurries across the room to the door to the kitchen. Army moves behind the front counter and crouches below the open drawer of a dusty cash register. I sneak behind the lunch counter press myself up against the shelves at the end where the counter faces the door.

"Go fuck yourself, Butcher," a woman that I presume to be Angel replies, and then the radio beeps again.

"Just shut it off," Pacho says again.

"Maybe I'll just keep it on so they can hear us doing it," Angel says.

"Fuck that," he says. "Gimme that."

There is a click and then it sounds like they start kissing just before the door to kitchen swings open. A woman with lots of tattoos on her arms and bright purple hair steps backwards into the room with her arms wrapped around a tall man with long black hair pulled back in a ponytail. Their eyes are closed as the continue back up and passionately grope and kiss each other until they are pressed up against the other side of the counter that I am crouched behind.

I lose sight of them when I duck my head down further, though they seem so involved in what they are doing that I doubt they would notice if I were to stand up right now.

I hear a belt buckle opening and a zipper being undone. Someone spits and then Pacho exhales loudly right as I hear a wet sucking noise.

It's not hard to imagine what is going on even though I am trying to avoid it.

Then I hear something else. It sounds like someone is choking. Blood spurts over the counter and splatters on the floor beside me.

"Pacho?" Angel gasps.

I lift my head up and see Pacho standing there, blood spurting from a gash in his throat. His eyes stare at the ceiling for a moment before he collapses to the floor, and I see Chase standing there behind him, gripping the bloody knife in his hand.

Angel tries to get off her knees and scream but Chase plasters his palm over her mouth and brings the bloody blade up so the sharp tip indents the tender skin of her neck.

"Shut the fuck up," he says. "You make even one sound I'll slit your goddamn throat, too."

Angel opens her eyes wide and starts to tremble uncontrollably. Her face and hair are drenched in blood.

"You hear me?" Chase says and applies a little more pressure on the knife, so it just breaks the skin and releases a small trickle of blood down her neck.

The woman nods her head anxiously.

"Get my bag," Chase says. "Bring it here."

I am light-headed from not breathing through all of this. I am still trying to wrap my mind around what just happened, but I move across the room, pick up the bag, and bring it to Chase.

"I don't want to hurt you," he tells Angel.

"What are you doing?" I ask him as I hand him the bag. He doesn't take it because he is still using his arms to restrain Angel.

"Don't worry about it," Chase says. "In there is a roll of tape. Get it."

I open the bag, dig around, find a roll of duct tape, and hand it to him.

"Get her wrists, damn it," he says.

I am still not sure what in the hell I am doing. Angel mumbles something into the palm of hand covering her mouth.

"Shut the fuck up," Chase growls at her.

Tears stream down her cheeks and her eyes plead with me not to do it but I wrap the duct tape tightly around her wrist several times. Chase puts the knife down on the counter as soon as I finish.

"Give me that," he says and snatches the roll of tape from my hands.

He takes his other hand off the woman's mouth for a second to pull a piece of tape off the roll.

"Please just let me go," Angel says softly. "You don't—"

Chase quickly shoves the tape hard into her mouth so that it pulls her cheeks back and prevents her from closing her mouth. She starts to struggle then. He wraps the roll around her head several times as she thrashes and turns from side to side. Finally, he gets her bound and then she just sort of submits and he lets go of her again.

"Just chill the fuck out," he tells her. "I promise I'm gonna let you go Angel, okay."

"We still good out there?" Chase asks Army.

Army looks out the window in both directions and then turns back to look at Chase and nods his head without a word. I can tell by the way he keeps looking at Angel that he is feeling as uncertain about all this as me.

"Good," Chase tells him. "Come over here."

Chase fishes through his bag again and pulls out a grenade.

"Hold on, Chase," I say. "What the hell are we doing here?"

"Blake," Chase says. "That big dead motherfucker on the floor is going to wake up any minute. I don't have time for your bullshit right now, so shut the fuck up and do what I say so we can all get out of this situation alive."

He pauses to grab the tape off the counter again."

"I'm sure Angel would like us all to get out of this alive too," he says and manages something that resembles a smile. "Right, Angel?"

Angel sobs silently nods her head slowly.

"Take the laser pointer in my bag," Chase tells Army. "Put the dot someplace only Tim can see it. Then both of you get behind the counter."

Chase glances down at the dead man in a puddle of blood on the floor to make sure he still isn't moving. Then he places the grenade in Angel's shaking hands and starts to wrap them with tape again. Angel starts to shake her head and whimper behind the layers of tape covering her mouth.

"Chase," I beg. "Hang on."

The dead man on floor moans and lifts his head off the floor slowly. Chase grabs his knife off the counter and walks Angel to the front door of the restaurant.

"No time," Chase says. "Get the fuck behind the counter. I got this."

He cuts the tape off from Angel's mouth. Then he pulls the pin out of the grenade and shoves it in her mouth when she tries to scream.

"Fuck," I curse. I don't know what the fuck he is doing but there is nothing I can do about it now.

"Listen to me," Chase says to Angel. "You have time to make it to them."

He points at the men by the basketball court.

"They can put the pin back. Don't try to stop or your boyfriend..."

He glances back at Pacho shambling around the counter with his pants around his ankles. Chase releases her just as Pacho reaches out to grab her and stumbles over his pants. She pushes open the door and the weight of Pacho knocks her back onto the sidewalk. Angel runs into the street toward the basketball court screaming with the grenade pin clenched in her teeth.

She gets about ten feet away from them when the grenade explodes. Pieces of shrapnel pelt the building and shatter the windows. Immediately following the blast, a barrage of gunfire erupts in the street.

Chase stands up and immediately opens fire through the shattered window at the men near the high school entrance. After only a few seconds, all the shooting stops.

"Clear," Chase says.

I get off the floor and look around.

The two men by the high school entrance lie motionless in the road. Smoke drifts up from a lit cigarette sitting on the ground beside their bodies.

Tim and Elise are standing over the dead men on the street by the smoldering fire in the trash can. Another man hangs from the gun turret, his blood still spilling down the passenger side windows.

Pieces of Angel are all over the road. The thing that used to be Pacho is mangled but trying to get back up off the ground. One of the men by the basketball court looks to be dead, but the other drags his body across the ground. His lower body seems unable to move and he leaves a trail of fresh blood as he tries to crawl away.

We walk through the door of the cafe and Chase heads straight for the injured guy. He lifts his rifle halfway up and squeezes the trigger without slowing his pace and puts a round through the skull of Pacho. Then he continues toward the injured man on the basketball court.

"Hold on," Tim says. "Don't shoot him."

Chase uses the toe of his boot to flip the man over roughly. Then he steps on the man's hand when he tries to reach for the gun on his belt.

Tim breaks into a run to reach us before anything else happens.

"Let's see what he knows," Tim says.

CHAPTER
TWENTY-SIX

"That really looks like it hurts," Chase says. He presses the toe of his boot on a shrapnel wound on the guy's chest.

The man howls in agony until Chase removes his foot. Tim nudges Chase aside and stares down at the sniveling man on the ground.

"Please," the man begs. "Please!" Whether he is begging for us to help him, let him go, or put him out of his misery is unclear.

"Do you know what happened to the people that attacked the castle the other night?" Tim asks

"Please," the man begs again. He doesn't even seem to be listening to a word Tim says.

"Are they alive?" Tim asks.

"Come on man," the guy says and clutches at the dirt with his filthy blood-crusted hands. "Please!"

"That's never gonna get him talking," Chase says.

"Just let me handle this," Tim says.

He crouches down on one knee beside the man and grabs his jaw until the man makes eye contact with him.

"Listen," Tim says. "There was a man and a woman."

"I don't know what you're talking about," the man says. "Please."

"Damn it," Tim sighs. He gets back up and looks at Chase for a moment. Then he turns his back and takes a few steps away.

Chase takes that as the signal to have at it, so he walks back over to the man and grabs a fistful of his dark sweaty hair. Chase pulls his head up so that his eyes are looking at the bodies down the road that are starting to get to their feet.

"You see them? I'm gonna level with you," Chase says. "You're already dead, man. So, you can stop all that goddamn begging."

"No! No!" the man cries.

"Shhh. I know it's hard to hear," Chase says. "But those are the facts. You just have to decide how bad it is going to be for you."

The man panics and hyperventilates as he stares up at Chase.

"You can tell us what we want to know, and I can make it painless for you," Chase says. Then he points a finger up the road. "Or I can leave you here with them."

The man starts to shake as he stares at the fresh corpses of his companions shambling toward him.

"Don't leave me," the man stammers.

"Tell me," Chase says. "Tell me what I want to know."

"We only killed one of them," the man says. "A blonde girl. Found her about a mile away the next day."

Chase hesitates for a second. Then he pulls the man by hair a little harder and talks through his clenched teeth.

"What about the others?" Chase asks him. "Are they still alive?"

"We only found two others. We caught a guy just outside the castle. Another woman was picked up in the woods," he pants. "They took them both alive."

Tim turns around when he hears this information.

"Are they still alive?" Tim says.

"Probably. I don't know," the man says.

Chase yanks his hair roughly.

"Shit, man!" the guy yells. "They would keep them alive until they got information about you."

That sounds exactly like what we're doing right now.

The other man that was on the court with him moans behind us and opens his eyes. He sits up and I can see one half of his face was badly mutilated in the blast. The other two corpses are near the entrance of the cafe and slowly advancing toward us.

"I swear I don't know anything else," the man says.

"Let's go," Tim says. He turns and starts to walk back toward the narco tanks where Elise is searching the dead bodies for ammo.

Chase releases the handful of hair in his grip and stands up. He stares down at the man for a moment. Then he reaches down and picks up the pistol next to the man and takes out the full magazine from the plate carrier the man is wearing.

"Please," the man begs him again. "Do it."

"Sorry bud," Chase says. "I can't spare the bullets."

The man grabs at his leg as Chase walks away. Then he turns and pleads to me with desperate eyes that quickly shift from my face to the approaching corpses.

"You guys promised!" the man yells. "Don't leave me like this!"

I hear shoes scraping the ground and turn to see Army leaving as well. The man says something in Spanish to Army, but Army just glances down for a moment and continues walking.

My hand moves to grip the barrel of my rifle. I take aim at his head but can't bring myself to pull the trigger. Killing has never been easy for me, but it isn't about that this time. When I stare down the sight, I don't see that guy there. I see Danielle. I see the faces of all the other people that died because of these men. They never got any mercy, so it doesn't feel right showing him any either.

"Fuck."

"What are you doing, man?" the guy says.

The dead are closing in around us. I know I can't stand here any longer, so I leave him and walk toward the car. He pleads with me for a few seconds longer, but I refuse to look back. His words soon turn to screams and cries of agony.

I realize now how different I am from the man I used to be. I don't think the old me could have just walked away like that. I might have been too afraid to pull that trigger before. I mean, as much as I hate him, I couldn't bring myself to shoot Chase. This was not about being afraid to hurt him. Leaving this man to die like was purely vindictive.

Part of me is afraid that I am becoming something else. Something like Chase. Maybe that is why the sight of him standing in the road suddenly fills me with rage.

"We'll take their trucks," Tim says. "Draw less attention that way."

"Fifty-cal might come in handy, too," Chase says.

"What the hell was that back there?" I say to Chase.

"What?" Chase says.

"That woman," I say. "You killed her."

"Oh, come on," Chase says.

"We don't have time for this," Tim interrupts.

"He taped a goddamn grenade in her hands," I say. "We can't be like this. Blowing up women like we're some kind of terrorists."

Tim turns and looks at Chase. I can tell this doesn't sit right with him either, but right now Tim is more concerned with finding his brother than anything else.

"I just did what had to be done," Chase says.

"You're crossing lines you can't uncross," Tim says.

"We're heavily outnumbered," Chase says. "I don't like it either but we're the insurgents now. You've been in the field. You know what that means. We can't keep our hands clean. Not if we're going to live."

"I have seen the cartel do things that are much worse," Army says.

"Tim," I say. "Are you really okay with this?"

"No!" Tim snaps. "No, I'm not okay with any of this. Okay? I just want to find my brother. Whatever it takes."

Tim storms away and circles around to open the door of the narco tank.

"Let's get moving," Tim says. "We've already wasted too much time here."

Chase climbs into the passenger seat with Tim. Elise and Army head for the other truck. Standing in the middle of these bullet riddle bodies, I watch the corpse ripping a human being apart. I need to look at the carnage in the street one more time to confirm that it is as horrific as I claimed and that I am not overreacting.

Tim starts the engine and starts to drive away.

"Come on, homie," Army says from the open door of the other vehicle.

I shove empty beer cans onto the floor and climb into the back seat that is covered in stains and cigarette burns and smells like mold and urine. As disgusting as it is, it still doesn't make me feel any dirtier after what just happened back there. When I close the sliding side door of the van, Elise shifts the engine into drive and hits the gas.

Army turns around in his seat to look at me. His eyes narrow as he scrutinizes me for several seconds.

"I'm okay," I tell him.

"No, homie," he says. He turns his head back around and stares at the road in front of us again. "None of us are okay anymore. That's just the way it is now."

I think about his words for a minute as I stare out the front window at the trunk of the armored SUV in front of us. After hearing him say it like that, I realize it is a feeling I've had for a while but haven't quite been able to put it into words.

Nobody is all right now.

It's been a long time since I have been around anyone that was acting normal. When people aren't just trying to stay alive, the only thing they seem to do is stare off into space for hours or sleep restlessly until the nightmares wake them up.

The last time I felt like that was when I was sitting on the train. I used to get irritated when I saw someone doing typical or annoying things like picking their nose or listening to shitty music too loud. Now, I'd give anything to go back to that world. But there is no going back.

"I just killed three people," Elise says. "Three living, breathing people. I never had to hurt anyone before. Even in the military."

I look at the mirror and see her eyes filling up with tears.

"I don't know how to deal with that," she says.

"You just live with it because it's better than being dead," I say.

"It's not going to be the last time. Eventually, you will get used to it," Army says.

"I don't want to get used to it," Elise says.

"I'm sorry, kid," I say. "Sometimes there really aren't any good choices if you want to stay alive."

CHAPTER
TWENTY-SEVEN

After we drive several miles up the mountain, we come to a lake along the left side of the highway. Several men stand around in the parking of the lakeside campground loading big water jugs in and out of truck trailers. They glance over at the narco tanks passing but don't detect anything out of the ordinary. Luckily, the blood from the guy that was in the turret is on the passenger side of the vehicle driven by Tim.

Still, it's just a matter of time before one of the Reaper patrols rolls through town and finds the bodies we left behind. Whatever we're going to do, we need to do it soon if we want to take them by surprise.

Above the treetops, the tower rising above the castle comes into view down the road. We pass a brown sign that, as much as I can tell, says that Bishop Castle is two miles ahead. The sign was covered in graffiti of the Grim Reaper and the blood dripping down from several human heads on spikes mounted on top as a warning. It's effective. Under other circumstances, it would be enough to make me head back the way I came.

I try not to look at it too closely but feel like I need to make sure that none of those heads look familiar to me.

Tim slows down in front of us and pulls off the road onto a gravel driveway of a heavily wooded property. He steers slowly around a curve and stops in front of a ramshackle building with a roof that collapsed long ago by the look of it.

We exit the vehicles and grab our weapons and as much ammo as we can carry.

"Don't take the keys. Leave them in the vehicles," Tim says to Elise.

She looks unsure but leans back inside and puts the key in the ignition. It takes a moment for me to understand the reason behind it too. If one of us takes the keys along, there is the possibility that person won't make it back here alive. It's not an outcome I like to think about but leaving the keys does make sense.

Clouds creep over the mountains and blanket the late afternoon sky as we hike through the trees in the direction of the castle. The wind starts to pick up again and brings with it the scent of a coming snowstorm. It's an indescribable scent that doesn't exist except when my body detects slight changes in the humidity and slowing speed of the molecules in the air. and then when I breathe the cold, moist air something in my brain concludes that I can smell the snow coming.

These distracting thoughts are comforting to me. If I feel like I under-stand the way the world works, then I can convince myself that it's in my power to control what happens in it. Thinking about things that I know keeps my mind off all the things that I don't know right now.

I don't like going into a situation when I know the odds of survival are this low. I may have beaten the odds many times before now, but others haven't been so lucky. The law of statistical regularity dictates that it will happen to me eventually, too. I just don't know when.

Damn it.

There I go. Worrying about the things I don't know yet again.

"Hold up," Tim whispers and raises a hand up to tell us to stop. His eyes scan the woods quickly and then his gaze returns to the ground. "Don't move."

"Shit," Chase curses.

"You didn't think to mention this before?" Tim says. He crouches down on the ground and picks up a twig while he surveys the land around us.

"I didn't see any out here," Chase says.

"What is it?" I whisper.

"Landmine," Tim says and points to a small piece of metal poking out beneath the dirt and leaves on the ground. "Homemade by the looks of it."

"We have to assume that ain't the only one out here," Chase says.

"Right," Tim says. He pokes the broken twig into the dirt, stands up, and adjusts the rifle strap on his shoulder. "Everybody keep close and watch your step."

We push forward through the trees again as the cloudy sky grows darker and the sun sinks into the horizon. It isn't long before we come across another trap. A tripwire hooked up to a claymore mine.

Twenty yards further we discover another device. This time it isn't an explosive at all. It's one of those big metal bear traps with jagged teeth, and it is just sitting out in the open. It's easy enough to see during the day, but we won't have any daylight much longer. As much as we don't want to get careless trying to hurry through the woods, it will be much more dangerous to be out here in the dark.

After I turn around and start walking again, I can't help but take one more look back at the scruffy dog and wonder if I will ever see him again.

We're close enough now to smell the smoke from the fires burning near the castle. Through the trees we can see the lights flicker as dusk falls. We emerge from the trees on a ridge above the castle back of the castle.

"Stop here for a minute," Tim says.

"Oh, thank god," Army says. He drops his weapon and backpack on the ground, collapses against a boulder, and slumps down to the ground. He gasps for air and swipes the sweaty hair off his brow with his forearm.

"You alright?" I ask him.

He still hasn't caught his breath enough to talk but he nods his head.

Tim takes out the binoculars and searches the grounds. He stops for a moment then adjusts the focus of the lenses and stares for another minute. Finally, he lowers the binoculars and hands them to Chase.

Chase only looks through them for a few seconds before handing them back.

"You see those tanker trucks down there?" Tim asks.

I reach for the binoculars to get a look for myself. It's too far from up here to see much without them.

The castle doesn't look like what I expected. It is more like what a castle might look like in a terrifying nightmare. Wrought iron balconies circle around the stone exterior with what look to be dead bodies hanging from them. A sniper lurks in the tower, watching over the perimeter beside a spotlight that scans the tree line.

In front of the castle there is a cage where a small crowd is gathered and cheering on two men fighting inside. To the left of the castle, a barbwire fence enclosure holds a herd of people like cattle waiting to be slaughtered. The whole place glows red from all the burning fires and clouds of smoke. I locate the trucks that Tim mentioned and then quickly pass the binoculars to Elise.

"What do you got in mind?" Chase asks.

"Scorched earth," Tim says. "At least one of those tankers has to have some fuel down there. First, we get one of us down there. Dump the fuel and start a big fire along the road. That will distract them. Get them scrambling. Then we'll make our move. The traps they set in the woods will work against them. Box them in."

"That's not bad," Chase says. "It might even work."

"It will work," Tim says. "You think you can get to the trucks?"

"I'll burn this whole damn place to the ground," Chase says.

"We can't," Elise says. "There are innocent people down there. They'll be trapped, too."

"We're going to let them all out," Tim says. "If our people are here, that's where we're going to find them. Between the fire and the prisoners being released, there will be enough chaos to locate our people and get the hell out."

"And what about the rest of the prisoners?" I say.

Tim looks silently at all the people locked up below, but he doesn't answer at first.

"Collateral damage," says Chase.

"No," says Tim. "By opening those gates up, we're giving them a chance to get out of there alive. They're as good as dead if they stay in there otherwise."

It makes sense, but it still doesn't make us feel any better about it.

"What's our exfil?" Chase says.

"Through the woods," Tim says. "Same way we came in. I marked our route, so we won't get lost or stumble into any traps in the dark."

We stare over the treetops at the burning lights and the ominous looking castle in silence for a minute as night descends.

"We ready then?" Chase finally says.

"You sure you can handle the fuel by yourself?" Tim asks.

"I work better alone," Chase says.

Tim watches Chase walk into the trees and disappear in the darkness and then he shakes his head and puts his binoculars back in his bag. He gets back to his feet and waits for the rest of us to get ready to move again as the first flakes of snow start to drift down from the sky around us and disappear when they come to rest the darkened earth.

CHAPTER TWENTY-EIGHT

We crouch in the shadows beyond the reach of the spotlight in the castle tower. I check my weapon one last time to make sure I have a full magazine and the safety is off. Everything is set. Now we just need to finish it.

The snow begins to collect on the ground as we wait. It seems like Chase is taking an eternity to ignite the fuel. Every minute that passes makes me worry even more that something may have happened to him.

"You see Chuck anywhere?" Elise whispers.

Tim shakes his head.

"Not any of them," he says. "They have to be in there somewhere."

A massive fireball suddenly erupts into the black sky. Even across the camp I can feel the wave of heat rushing over me a few seconds later.

"Jesus," Tim says.

"You said scorched earth," Army says.

Inside the compound, the men in the middle of the cage stop fighting. Everyone standing outside the ring stares at the blaze in shock. The only sound for several seconds after that is the roar of the flames.

"Wait," Tim tells us.

A shrill scream pierces the air. Seconds later a man covered in flames comes sprinting from the direction of the fire. He collapses on the ground and continues burning.

Another fireball lights up the night. This time it comes from a shipping container on the other side of the camp. A lot of smaller explosions follow. It almost sounds like fireworks. The trailer must have been their ammo dump or something.

I have to hand it to Chase; he certainly got their attention.

Panic erupts. The men surrounding the cage start to run. Some of them head for the fire and some run from it instead. The prisoners start to gather along the fence and shake the gates.

Tim fires off a shot and I look up to see the sniper in the tower topple over the edge and plummet to the ground.

"Now," Tim says.

We break from the cover of the woods and Tim leads us along the side of the castle. Tim lifts his rifle and opens fire on a pair of sentries on the second-floor balcony of the castle.

With all the explosions and chaos, no one seems to react to the sound of the gunfire right away. The guards are so distracted yelling at the prisoners trying to break down the fence that they don't even notice us coming at them until it's too late.

I take a shot at the guard in front of the gates and hit him in the chest. Then I take out another guy with a pistol that starts shooting at us from on top of a lookout tower at the corner of the enclosure.

Tim uses his rifle stock to smash the lock on the prison gates. Army and Elise turn to cover his back while he tries to release the captives.

It doesn't take long for us to be noticed now. Bullets zip through the air near my head. None of us get hit, but the people crowding against the other side of the fence aren't so lucky. Elise and Army return fire and hit several Reapers coming at us from the entrance of the castle.

Tim gets the lock off and we open the gates. The people nearly trample us as the rush forward. A few of them stop to grab the weapons off the dead bodies lying on the ground and fight. Others just run for the woods to

"Chuck!" Tim yells.

He searches the faces of the people shoving their way out of the fence. As the last few prisoners make their way out of the enclosure, Tim stops searching for his brother.

Among the bodies on the ground, there is a woman with dark hair lying face down that looks like Scout.

"Scout!" I say.

I kneel beside her and turn her over to discover Stevie cowering and shivering in the mud.

Scout moans slightly and then I look down and see the blood on her white shirt. The bottom of one leg of her jeans is coated in blood as well. I can't really tell how bad either injury is, but she is at least coherent for now.

"She's hurt," I say.

"Put pressure on that," Tim instructs me.

He crouches down beside me and shrugs his pack off. He pulls out some kind of nylon strap with a plastic buckle from his bag. Then I realize what he is holding is a tourniquet. He quickly tightens it around her leg.

"Where's Fletcher?" Tim asks her.

"They took him," Scout winces. "Inside."

"Elise!" Tim yells. "Army!"

The fire has reached the trees and is spreading quickly. People are coughing from the overwhelming smoke. One of the countless mines in the forest explodes behind us. I start to get the feeling that this is going to be it for us all. We're all going to die here.

"You guys get Scout and the kid out of here," Tim says. "I'm going to find my brother."

I help get Scout up and help Army move her, but then I remember the promise I made to Stacy. Now, I understand what she was worried about. I don't think Tim will leave here without his brother even if that means that he doesn't get out of here alive.

I look up and watch as he storms toward the entrance of the castle without even looking back or seeming to notice the bullets flying in the air around him.

"You got her?" I ask Army.

He nods his head and then I let go of her.

Bullets tear up the dirt next to me as I run to catch up to Tim. I turn and spray bullets blindly into the haze. My eyes are so watery from the smoke that I can barely see as it is. I stumble over a dead body on the ground and then notice it starts to move again.

It grabs my arm and opens its jaws. A second later, a bullet obliterates the dead man's head, and it falls back to the ground. Tim bends down and grabs my arm to help me get to my feet again.

We scramble beneath the stone archway on the ground floor of the castle. Tim fires several rounds behind him and then takes cover behind the stone wall. Bullets patter the other side of the wall, sending bits of rocks flying on impact.

"What are you doing?" Tim yells. "I told you to get out of here."

"I'm coming with you," I tell him.

As bad as this situation is right now, it is about to get much, much worse. Once the dead rise this is going to turn into a real bloodbath. We don't want to be here when that happens.

I take the opportunity to switch out my empty mag. Tim notices a rope on the wall beside him. He looks up and spots a metal gate above the entrance and then he releases the rope, and the metal gate drops down and slams against the floor.

A few second later, I hear more gunshots behind me. I spin back around and see two guys in men fall down the staircase across the hall.

"Chuck!" Tim yells as he marches ahead toward the staircase.

He takes out the magazine from his rifle and reloads as he walks past a statue of a skeleton in black robe. It holds a scythe in one hand and a skull in the other. The only light in the room comes from the flickering candles burning amongst the offerings of gold, blood-covered money and human bones piled on the floor.

I run up the steps behind him and emerge from the staircase into a cavernous room. The only light is the glow from the blaze outside coming through the stained-glass windows all around us.

A match ignites in the darkness and in the glow, we see a man with long, black hair and a skeleton tattooed on his face lighting a cigar. He waves out the match and then all only his silhouette and the faint orange glow of the tip of his cigar can be seen in the darkness.

"It's over, Castillo," Tim says.

"You know me?" Castillo says. His voice sounds calm and raspy with a pronounced accent.

"Oh, I know you," Tim says. "Where is my brother?"

The glowing cigar tip makes a circular motion and then an overhead light flicks on in the back of the room. A man sits in a chair beneath the glow of the light. His head hangs down until a hand comes out of the darkness and grabs him by the hair and pulls his head back to reveal his swollen bruised fast. Another hand comes out of the darkness and presses the blade of a machete against his neck.

I should have known we wouldn't find Castillo alone and unarmed up here. It is never that easy. I scan the dark corners of the room but there is really no way to know how many of them could be lurking in here. I raise my rifle at keep the barrel pointed at the man with the machete.

Outside the fire rages, smoke fills the sky. The shooting begins to taper off but now the moans of the dead grow louder.

"Here I am trying to get this man to tell me where to find you and you bring yourselves to me like a gift," he says.

"Let him go, Castillo," Tim says.

He sucks the cigar for several seconds and in the glow, I can see his eyes staring at Tim the whole time.

"Fletcher," Castillo says. "Now I remember you."

He exhales a cloud of smoke into the air that is faintly visible as it swirls in the moonlight. He must be a real lunatic to be this calm with everything that is going on outside.

"This is quite a special gift," Castillo says.

A small red dot flashes on Castillo's chest. He doesn't seem to notice as it blinks on and off continuously as he talks.

"You won't feel that way in a few minutes," Tim warns him.

"This can't be coincidence," Castillo says. "God has brought you to me to face your fate. You will join the rest of your men whose souls belong to me now."

"Yeah," says Tim. "I guess we'll see about that."

Castillo takes another long drag off his cigar and laughs starts to laugh. Tim smirks and starts to laugh to. I start to wonder if everyone around me has gone completely insane. I am also still trying to look around and figure out where that red spot is coming from.

"You don't have the power to stop me," he says. "I am protected by God! I am Death!"

Glass suddenly shatters and a bottle with a burning rag sticking out of the top flies across the room. I instinctively squeeze the trigger with my gun still aimed at the man holding the machete to Chuck's neck. A split-second later it feels like I get hit in the chest with a baseball bat.

Before I hit the floor, I see muzzles flashing all around the room. Then hear the chaos of gunfire and bullets hitting the stone walls and shattering the stained glass.

The flying bottle hits Castillo and shatters and spews fire across the wooden floorboards. The burning man steps back toward the windows. He howls and waves his arms wildly while firing his pistol blindly. Tim crouches beside me and fires several times, hitting him in the chest and staggering him farther backwards. Finally, he crashes through the glass and falls to the ground below.

"Clear," Chase walks into the room from the balcony to my right. He slowly lowers his rifle and stares at the hole in the stained-glass window across the room.

Tim glances at Chase and then lowers his rifle as well. He turns his head and checks me over.

"You okay?" Tim says.

"I think," I say.

Tim gets up and runs across the room to check on his brother.

I sit up and tuck my hand beneath the flak jacket to check the painful spot in my chest. It hurts like hell to breathe. When I take my hand out there is a splotch of red blood on my fingers.

"I'm hit," I say.

Chase shoulders his weapon and reaches over and checks my chest beneath the vest. I wince and cry out from the sharp pain when his fingers search for my wound.

"Is it bad?" I ask him.

"You're fine," Chase says. "It didn't even go through."

"I'm bleeding," I say.

"You have some abrasions from force," Chase says. "Maybe some cracked ribs. You'll be fine, but we won't be if we don't get the fuck out of here."

He helps me to my feet and then we walk over to the window. Below us, the undead are tearing into the scorched flesh of La Parca. They rip out his intestines and gnaw on his charred arms and legs.

"Protected by God, my ass," Chase says. "Adios, muchacho." He spits out the window at the dead man before he turns away from the window and crosses the room.

I look down at Castillo once more and see the blood splatters on the morbid skull tattoo covering his face. His eyes stare up blankly at the sky and then he disappears forever beneath the horde of the dead.

Tim helps Chuck out of the restraints. Chuck barely has the strength to get to his feet, so Tim lifts his brother's arm around his own shoulder and helps him to walk.

The fire from the Molotov cocktail is rapidly spreading and every few seconds one of us has to cough from the smoke.

"We need a way out," Tim says. "Chase..."

"Over here," says Chase.

We climb back out through the window that Chase shattered when he entered and step onto a thin wooden ledge. We move to the corner of the castle where there is a long thin stone stairway with no railing or anything at all on the sides. No wonder the dead couldn't get up this way.

I am not sure how Tim is going to be able to help Chuck get down without either of them falling, but we have to try.

CHAPTER
TWENTY-NINE

Chase leads the way as we descend the stairs into the swirling smoke and moaning dead that lurk below. I watch nervously as Tim helps Fletcher carefully down each step ahead of me.

At least nobody is shooting at us now, but that is probably because the only people left around here are dead.

For a few moments, the corpses don't even seem to notice us. I really still don't know how good their senses are to begin with, but with all the smoke in the air and the crackling roar of the burning trees around us, we make it halfway down before the dead start moaning and clambering at the wall of stone beneath us.

Chase opens fire at a severely burned man that tries to walk up the stairs. The bullet hits him in the skull and knocks him off the stairs. Chase shifts the barrel of his rifle and fires repeatedly as he walks down the stairs to clear a path for us to escape through the dead. The gunfire attracts the attention of every corpse surrounding the castle.

I lift my rifle and aim into the horde below, but the recoil against my bruised ribs hurts like hell and the tears that flood my vision aren't entirely from the smoke. I fight through the pain and keep shooting even though I am probably wasting most of my bullets.

"Gimme a gun!" Fletcher yells at Tim as loudly as he can, but I can barely hear his voice over all the noise.

Tim reaches to his hip holster and removes his pistol. He hands it to Fletcher who slowly raises it with his exhausted arm and fires into the snarling faces of the dead.

Tim grips the handle of rifle and sprays bullets into the crowd of bodies as he fires from hip. While the bullets aren't stopping the dead, we manage to drop enough of them and push them back to open a path at the bottom of the steps for us to make a run for it.

By the time we get down there, each of us is out of bullets in our magazine. We shove the dead away as they swarm around us and make a break for the woods. Fletcher still drags his feet along the ground and even with Tim helping him along, they don't move much faster than the dead.

Chase manages to swap to a fresh mag while he navigates through the dead. He fires at anything that comes at us from the front, only stopping to shove a corpse down that comes at us from the side.

I try to hold off the dead behind us but start to fall behind when I walk backwards, and I am afraid of losing sight of them in this smoke every time

I turn around. The last thing I need is to end up out here on my own right now with all hell breaking loose.

We make it to the woods and start up the incline. The brief relief I felt about being away from the blazing heat of the burning castle is gone as soon as I notice the cracking twigs and the shambling shapes moaning in the dark all around us. The dead are walking all through the woods now too.

A figure rushes at me through the tree branches to my left. I pivot and fire at the thing but only hit it a couple times in the chest. It knocks into my rifle and the stock jabs me hard in the chest. The blow lands right in the spot I took the bullet a few minutes ago. I still manage to fend him off with the rifle and then when he falls to the snowy ground, I point the barrel at the dark shape of its' skull and shoot it pointblank in the face.

I try to take a deep breath, but my ribs make it so painful, and the fire seems to have consumed all the oxygen in the air, so I still feel unable to breathe. My legs start to feel tired, and I wonder for a second if I'm going to pass out. If that happens, I know I won't be making it home.

"Go," I tell myself. "You have to go."

Somehow, I dig down and get my legs moving. I look up the hill and can still see the guys up ahead, but I am already too far behind them.

A raspy moan and rustling branches tell me another corpse is coming at me. I don't have time to look and see where it is. If I just keep moving it won't catch up to me.

Then I hear a distinctive click in the darkness.

An explosion sends soil, chunks of wood and human tissue flying at me. The blast sends me sprawling on the ground. My ears ring. The entire world spins for several seconds as I lay in the dirt and wonder if I am dead.

When I finally get to my hands and knees and shake my head to try and get it working again, I look around and in the flickering light from the fire, I see the dead coming at me from every direction.

I try to get to my feet, but my balance is so terrible that I fall forward toward the ground. Seconds later, fingers wrap around my arm, and I barely find the strength to shrug my arm free.

"Get the fuck up, man," Chase yells.

He fires at the dead surrounding us with his pistol and holds out his hand with the missing fingers to help me up. I stare at it for a moment because my brain has trouble making sense of everything right now. I'm still not even sure if he is here right now or if my rattled brain is completely broken.

"Come on!" Chase screams.

I finally grab his hand and he pulls me to my feet. I wobble unsteadily but manage to put one foot in front of the other and keep a grip on Chase as he helps me through the woods.

"You came back for me?" I ask Chase.

"Quiet," Chase whispers.

I'm not even sure how loud I am talking because my ears are still ringing."

"I wouldn't leave your dumb ass to die out here like that," he laughs. "I might have thought about it though."

The rest of the walk back to the car is a slow shuffle through the gathering snow. We catch up with Tim and Fletcher and follow his trail of broken sticks back to the cabin where we parked the vehicles.

There is no sign of the van except for the tire tracks left behind in the snow. The sport-utility vehicle remains where we left it.

"Looks like they made it out," Tim says.

"Looks like it," Chase agrees as he climbs behind the steering wheel. He starts up the engine and we all sit in our seats for a moment watching the fire raging on the horizon. Smoke drifts up the sky and the orange glow lights up the night.

"Let's go home," Tim says.

Chase turns on the headlights, shifts the vehicle into reverse, and backs down the driveway. In the mirror on the passenger side visor, I see my face. One side of it is covered in dirt and crusted blood that isn't mine. I'm not sure how or when it got there. I try to remember everything that happened leading up to this moment but much of it is still lost right now. The last thing I recall was going down the steps outside of the castle. So, I lay back in the seat and close my eyes and try to piece it together.

"Hey, bud," Chase says and taps me on the shoulder with his hand. "Don't go to sleep. You got your bell rung pretty good. Seems like you probably have a concussion."

"What?" I ask him.

"You hit your head," he says.

"No, I didn't," I say. I don't remember hitting my head at all. The fact that I don't remember anything may be a sign that he is right.

"Probably don't even remember me saving your ass either," he says.

"What?" I ask him.

"That figures," says Chase.

"Yeah. You definitely got a concussion," Chase says. "Just take it easy."

He turns and looks at me and for the first time he isn't staring at me like he hates my guts and I'm not sure what changed.

I turn around and look into the backseat and see Chuck laying back in his seat. Tim has the first aid supplies pulled out of the seat and he works on cleaning the cuts on his brother's face.

"How is he?" I ask Tim.

"Never better," Chuck mumbles. "Ow, you son of a bitch."

Tim withdraws his hand with the swab soaked in alcohol.

"Seems like he is just as much of a crybaby as ever," Tim says.

"They even tried zapping my nuts with a car battery, but it didn't cure me," Chuck says.

"Good to have you back brother," Tim says.

"Thanks for saving my ass," Chuck says.

"Don't mean to spoil the family reunion" Chase says. "But we don't have enough gas in this thing to make it back home."

The low fuel warning sound dings repeatedly in the silence that follows.

"Think we can get back to the Jeep?" Tim asks.

"Not looking like it," Chase says.

"Find a place we can stop to rest for a few hours," Tim says. "I'm going to have to crash for a couple of hours if we're going to hoof it."

"There's not much around here," Chase says.

"It doesn't matter where," Tim says. "Any spot that gets us out of sight of the road will work."

Chase pulls off the road a couple minutes later and drives beneath the wrought iron sign for a cemetery. In the glow of the headlights, I glimpse the badly damaged headstones resting in the overgrown grass. Chase steers down a gravel road towards a maintenance building at the edge of grave-yard.

"A cemetery?"

"Something wrong?" Chase asks.

"We're in a goddamn cemetery; That's what's wrong," Chuck says. "I know I look halfway dead, but I think you fellas are getting a little ahead of yourselves."

"If this is too scary, I can turn around," Chase laughs.

To hear everyone together and joking around once again makes me smile for the first time in what seems like forever.

"This is fine," Tim says.

Chase drives the car into the open garage of the maintenance building and puts it in park.

"We can lay low here for a couple hours and we'll find some transportation in the morning," Tim says.

I lay my head back and close my eyes and when I open them again the car is out of gasoline. The fuel warning tone goes quiet, the engine dies, and the warm air stops flowing through the air vents.

"Blake," Chase says. He sits in the seat next to me and seems to be watching me closely.

"What?" I say.

"You remember where we are?" he says.

"The cemetery," I say. "Why?"

"Just checking," he says. "You can go back to sleep."

CHAPTER THIRTY

As soon as the sun rises behind a veil of clouds and the bitter cold wakes us from sleep, we set out to figure out a way home. The snow has continued to fall for the last couple of hours and now there is nearly a foot of snow on the ground, which makes it even harder to walk on top of being utterly exhausted. If this snow doesn't let up, we may be able to drive through the snow or even see the highway to drive home.

Despite all of that, we are all still in relatively good spirits after the events of the previous night. Even Chase is still in a pleasant mood as we start trudging through the snow in the cemetery. Mostly, we all just want to get home and hope that we find everyone else made it back there safe as well.

Our biggest problem is that we're still probably more than fifty miles from the cabin and there is over a foot of snow on the ground. Even if we hike all the way back to town and get the Cherokee, driving on these roads might not be possible right now and it could be days before the temperature rises enough to melt the snow. At least I know the van that

Elise and Army drove had enough gas to make it to the cabin. I just hope they were able to make it through the snow.

"This reminds me of the day this all started," Chase says as we step through the partially buried tombstones. "My platoon was training out in Pickel Meadows. Hiking for miles through the mountains and sleeping in tents out in the snow."

"Sound like some real Girl Scout shit," Fletcher teases him.

"Fuck off," Chase says with a grin.

"You bake some cookies, too?" Tim says.

"Good one," Chuck laughs and elbows his brother gently.

I smile too, but I still don't feel comfortable joking around with Chase yet after everything that has happened between us before. I mean, I did come close to blowing his head off. Things might be different after everything we've been through now, but it'll still take some time for me to get used to it.

"It was cold as shit out there. I thought I hated it, but now, I guess it wasn't so bad," Chase says and then he pauses for several seconds. "Those guys were like family. My brothers. That was the last time we were all together. They flew us straight into Vegas from there. A few hours later most of the platoon was dead."

There is nothing really to say to that, so we just walk along silently around him.

"Being back in the snow reminds me of the last time life was only moderately fucked up and not completely FUBAR," he says. "It reminds me of the last time I was with my family. So even though I still hate the cold, I guess this ain't so bad, being out here."

"Well, aren't you just a ray of goddamn sunshine now," Fletcher says.

"I'm still cold as hell," Tim says. "We need to find us some transportation that can get us through that snow. I don't feel like hiking all the way back to the cabin."

"Yeah," I say. "I second that."

I'm not even sure that I could hike all the way. My ribs are still making me wince with every step and it's hard to breathe. At least I took a couple of painkillers that Tim gave me, and my headache is almost gone.

"We'll have to figure out something," Chuck says. "Driving around up here in the winter just isn't going to be possible. We need a plow or something."

After a couple of hours of hiking through abandoned farms, we're getting cold and tired. I am beginning to think that we should have stuck to the main highway. Even though it would make our trip twice the miles, we might have had better luck finding a way to get ourselves home quicker than this. We hardly talk since we are all breathing hard from hiking in the snow.

We spot a farm on the edge of a pond in the distance and start to head in that direction. As we approach, I see something that looks like a pasture fence sticking out of the snow. Upon closer inspection, I realize it's not a fence at all but the rails of an oval track for training racehorses.

"Look at that," Fletcher says and points towards the barn.

Half a dozen horses stand inside the giant doorway of the barn looking out at the snow. When they exhale their hot breath hangs in the air in front of their long faces.

"Keep your eyes open," Tim says. "Those horses belong to somebody."

We approach the farmhouse first and step cautiously onto the creaky porch. There are no footprints in the snow to indicate that anyone is still around. I cup my hands to the window and peer inside. The house is dark and dusty. On the kitchen floor is a shattered coffee cup and what looks like the remains of a small dead animal. It may be a dog or a cat.

"Looks like nobody has been home for a while," I say quietly.

Chase taps on the glass and then there is a moan and the sound of things crashing to the floor inside. A dead man in overalls shambles through the kitchen, stepping on the dead animal on the floor and knocking pots and dishes off the dusty countertop. It crashes against the other side of the front door and claws at the wood.

Tim turns and looks back at the barn. We walk back down the porch steps and head for the barn.

"Who in the hell is taking care of them then?" he says.

"They got water over there," Chase says. "They aren't locked up in the barn so they can go wherever they want."

"So instead of leaving they just stuck around here," Tim says.

"It's their home," I say.

"Look," Chuck says. He gestures to an old pickup parked by the garage with a flat tire. There is a plow attachment resting nearby in the grass.

"We might be able to get that truck started," Chuck says. "Can probably find another tire someplace around here."

"The truck? Why?" Chase says. "Just take the horses."

Chuck and Tim exchange uncertain glances. I don't even know how to ride a horse, but it might be the better option right now.

"That's not a bad idea," I say. "Fuel is already pretty hard to come by these days. It isn't going to get easier to find anytime soon."

The horses trot out of the barn when they see us approaching. They stand around in the snow and watch us from a distance.

"Isn't it going to be hard to like lasso them and all that?" Chuck asks.

"Lasso them?" Chase says. "Are you being serious right now?"

"I fly planes," Chuck says. "I don't know shit about horses."

"You're not allowed to wear that cowboy hat anymore," Chase says.

He walks through the barn doors and leaves us standing around staring at the haggard horses standing in front of the rundown track. I can't help but think back to the track back at home. I mean this place is a shithole in comparison, but the same goes for everything else in the world now too. Even us.

Chase returns a moment later with a harness and a bucket. He scoops out a handful of feed from the bucket and slowly approaches a horse. He holds out the food and lets the horse eat from his hand. Then he tosses one end of the lead rope over the strong neck of the horse gently and grabs the two pieces under his neck.

"Easy," he says as he pets the nose of the horse. Then he turns his head and I realize he wasn't saying that to calm the horse but to tell us how simple it is. He slips the harness over the horse's head and fastens it and then walks the horse over to the barn and ties him to the stall.

"How do you know so much about horses?" I ask him when he returns from the barn with another harness in his hands.

"There's a million horses in Texas," he says. "Pretty hard to grow up down there and not learn a thing or two about them."

Once all the horses are saddled, Chase shows us how to climb up on the horses and after a quick crash course we start riding home. Chase even decided to saddle up and lead the two other horses alongside him. He said these horses probably all stayed together because they were a herd. If we left one or two behind, they would keep anxiously searching for the others and might end up dead anyway, so it was best to just bring them all back with us anyway.

With Chase leading the way, the horses the rest of us ride seem content to just follow along, so it is easy for me to get the hang of it. My injured ribs being jostled around doesn't feel great, but I swallow another couple of painkillers to help manage the pain.

It takes me awhile to feel secure in the saddle, but then I start to like riding the horse. They are built by nature to be so powerful and yet they willingly allow others to ride on their backs. They even seem to get some sense of happiness from doing it. I spent all my time analyzing data and calculating statistics about horses to try and understand them. The truth is I never understood them at all before now.

We make good time by cutting through the national forest and make it back to Mount Blanca by the evening. We stop for a moment when we see the black SUV with the turret gun on top parked at the bottom of the trail to the cabin.

"Looks like they made it," Tim says. "That's a good sign."

While it is a good sign, all of us just want to get back up to the cabin and see if everyone is doing okay there. We head for the trail and ride the horses up the snowy mountain. We eventually make it up to the ridge and the black shimmering waters of the lake come into view. Behind it, the cabin with lights glowing in the window and a trail of smoke drifting up from the chimney into the dark starry sky.

As we approach the house, the door opens and Elise steps out onto the porch.

"It's them," She pokes her head back inside and doorway and yells. "Stacy! They're back! All of them!"

Bones steps outside as well and waits with her as our horses trot through the snow toward the cabin. We dismount and tie the leads to the railing on the porch for the moment. There isn't really a barn to keep the horses, but I suppose we have the time and resources to build one now.

Tim gives Elise and hurries inside to get to his wife and baby.

"Jesus, Chuck," Bones says when she gets a look at his swollen and bruised face.

"I'm fine. How is Scout?" he asks impatiently.

"She lost a lot of blood," Bones says. "But she is okay."

"Amanda?" I ask her.

"She is awake now," Bones tells me. "She's been worried about you."

I hurry inside to get out of the cold and see my wife. The inside of the house is warm and feels really crowded with everyone inside it again. It's a good feeling to see a room full of smiles.

I shrug off my coat beside Tim, who is hugging Stacy as she cries tears of joy.

"It's going to be okay now," he assures her. "We brought everybody home."

I put my coat on the rack by the door, head straight down the hallway, and walk through the open door to the bedroom. Stitch lifts his head when I walk in the room. Amanda stops petting him and looks at me and smiles.

"Hey," she says.

Right then, without even hearing her say anything else, I know that the two of us will figure our way through this together. I rush over to the side of the bed, bend down, and wrap my arms around her. Even though it hurts like hell to hug her right now, it isn't something that can wait until later.

"Are you feeling okay?" I ask her.

"I've been better," she says. "But I am okay."

"Listen," I say. "I'm sorry about the baby. I didn't want to risk losing you again. Maybe it was wrong, but—"

"Relax," she says and puts her hand over mine. "Everything is going to be okay."

EPILOGUE

I am sipping from a steaming cup of coffee while I watch the falling snow cover the forest floor on a frosty winter morning. It may be the end of the world, but that is even more reason to make the best of the time I have left here.

Chase walks by the window as he gets the horses ready outside. Stitch bounces around him in the snow until Chase bends down and picks up the ball and tosses it for Stitch. It seems like Chase has decided to stick around. Elise may have something to do with that. He might not be over losing Natalie, but he never seems too far away from Elise.

"You ready?" Scout says as she limps into the room. She has recovered well from her injuries, but her leg will take quite some time to heal after getting caught in one of the bear traps in the woods outside the castle.

"Almost done," I tell her.

"Fletcher wants to get on the road before we get too much snow."

"I'll be ready," I say.

Today we are moving ourselves to the store we secured in Pueblo. It might still be a long shot, but we think that will be our best chance of surviving the winter.

Tim and Stacy decided to stay here in the cabin. This is their home, and they want to keep little C.J. as far away from the dead as possible so he can have a somewhat normal childhood. Can't say I blame them.

I finish drinking the last of my coffee and when I set the cup down on the coffee table, I spot the copy of my book that Bones took from the bookstore lying there. I look at the stupid cover for a minute.

Writing it really does seem like such an irrelevant way to spend my time in hindsight. At the time, I thought it was so important I put aside everything else in my life to make money and prove how smart I was to everyone. Now, no one will ever need that information ever again.

My finger touches the smooth paperback cover and then I decide to pick it up with the intention of chucking it in the trash. But first, I flip through the pages one last time and stop on the afterword, which always seems the most useless part of any book. I don't even recall what it was that I wrote there anymore. I skim through the paragraphs and only stop when I read the last sentence.

What a bunch of crap. None of it matters now.

I used to think I could make sense of the world, but I have finally come to the conclusion that the world just doesn't make sense. We're just here until we aren't anymore.

I close up the book and stare at it once more. Then I reach down and open up my bag and shove it inside.

Amanda walks into the room and I get up from the chair and grab my bag off the floor.

"You got everything?" she says.

"Now I do," I tell her and grab her hand.

Amanda rolls her eyes at me and smiles and I finally feel like I made it home.

By definition, there are no happy endings in the apocalypse. We are all just running out of time, and I know my story will be no exception. But at least it isn't over yet.

THE END

Acknowledgments

This book, and really the entire series, would never have been possible without the patience and support of my amazing wife, and the cooperation of my two daughters. I truly appreciate the sacrifices they've made over the years to make it possible for me to create these stories. Also, thanks go to everyone that has read and supported this series along the way. There was a time I never thought I would finish writing one book. Because of your passion and encouragement, I have been lucky enough to continue working on creating more stories for the last five years. I truly appreciate each and every reader and can't wait for our next adventure together.

ABOUT THE AUTHOR

Jeremy Dyson is a fiction author who loves all things related to post-apocalyptic horror. He graduated from the University of Iowa where he studied English and dreamed of writing books one day. When he isn't writing he spends his time drinking beer, listening to metal, and gaming. He currently lives in Crystal Lake, Illinois with the love of his life, their two amazing daughters, and black goldendoodle named Duke. He is currently at work on another post-apocalyptic series.

amazon.com/Jeremy-Dyson/e/B01CZ41PIE/

facebook.com/jeremydysonauthor

instagram.com/jeremydyson

twitter.com/writerofthedead

♪

tiktok.com/jeremydysonauthor

For more information visit: **http://www.jeremydyson.com**

If you have enjoyed this book, please take a moment to **leave a review** to show your support for the author.

ALSO BY JEREMY DYSON

ROTD Series

RISE OF THE DEAD

RETURN OF THE DEAD

RAGE OF THE DEAD

REFUGE OF THE DEAD

REMNANTS OF THE DEAD

Printed in Great Britain
by Amazon

55673105R00162